THE CARSON CITY BRIDE

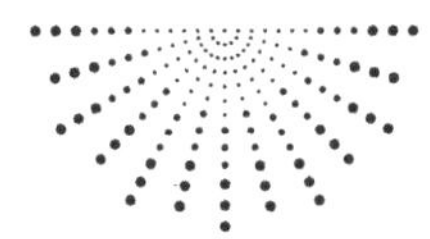

CYNTHIA WOOLF

Published by Firehouse Publishing
Woolf, Cynthia

CHAPTER ONE

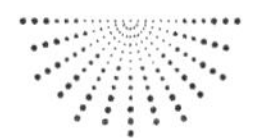

St. Joseph, Missouri – August 1861

At twenty-six Rachel Maitland had been a widow for a year. Now she watched a fresh pot of coffee boil on the stove in the kitchen she'd come to know so well. The room that had been her sanctuary away from her husband before he died.

Somehow she'd managed to live on the five hundred dollars remaining after all of Claude's assets were sold to pay his debts and she sold her ballgowns and evening dresses, twelve in all. She wouldn't need them where she was going and she would need the money they would bring. Claude's debts could be paid out of his assets, not hers. After nine years with him, she deserved to have what money her gowns brought. The sales had been for more than she imagined. She'd received four-hundred-fifty dollars for all twelve. A matron was buying them for her granddaughter's coming out. The woman had gotten a great deal. The gowns had originally cost Claude approximately three-hundred dollars apiece. Nothing was too good for Claude's wife.

Now that she was alone, she appreciated that he'd dressed her well. She'd have to wear the dresses she had for a long time. She was happy to know they were very well-made and would stand up over time.

But the money from the sale of Claude's assets was gone. She was lucky that the buyer of the house had allowed her to stay for minimal rent. He was a friend of hers, not Claude's, and wanted her to be safe. Now, however, he had to sell. He'd told her long ago that he would be.

Rachel was not one to sit and do nothing. Knowing she had no particular skills other than being a wife, she began a correspondence with a man in Carson City in the Nevada Territory. She was his mail-order bride and was leaving to go to him today. Everything she owned was now in two trunks in the hallway waiting for the freight company to pick them up.

Being a mail-order bride was the only thing she thought she could do. She figured if she could marry

Claude when she was sixteen and he was fifty-six, she could stand marriage to just about anyone. Mr. Johnson, her fiancé, was ten years older than she was and after Claude, he seemed a very young man to her.

As for Claude, she'd had no choice but to marry him. He'd bought her from her father.

A knock sounded on the front door.

That must be the freight wagon. "Coming." She called and hurried from the kitchen, putting her fears aside for a few moments.

She walked around her trunks standing neatly in the hall and answered the door. Two trunks and one carpetbag, that was all she had left after nine years of marriage.

Rachel opened the door wide. "Frank!" She engulfed her little brother in her arms. "I'm so glad you were able to come see me off."

He hugged her. "I couldn't let my big sis go off to get married without wishing her well." He pulled back and looked down at her from his five-foot, eight-,inch height. "I hope you find happiness this time, Rach."

"As do I. I can still offer you a cup of coffee if you'd like one. I just made a fresh pot with the last of the coffee. Everything else is gone."

"That would be great, if it's no trouble."

"None at all. I'll be right back."

As soon as his sister was out of sight, Frank opened the nearest trunk, dug to the bottom and made a slit in the lining. He pulled an envelope from inside his coat and placed it in the slit. Then he covered it again with her linens, closed the lid on the trunk and sat on it.

Rachel returned with two cups of coffee, handed him one and then sat on the second trunk. “When do you leave on your next Pony Express ride?”

“Today. I have to be back there in half-an-hour, but I wanted to say goodbye first. If I get to Carson City, I’ll look you up.” He sipped his coffee. “But I don’t usually ride that leg of the trip.”

“I’ll be happy to have you whenever you come.”

There was a knock on the front door.

“Excuse me, Frank.” She opened the door.

A man in overalls stood on the doorstep. “Mrs. Maitland?”

“Yes, I’m Rachel Maitland. I have the trunks ready for you.”

He tipped his hat.

She estimated he was in his forties from the thinning brown hair on top of his head.

“Yes, ma’am. I’m Mr. Von Glinski. I’ll drop you at the stage depot and take the trunks with me. I assume you want your carpetbag with you.”

“Yes, I do.” Rachel placed her hand on her brother's arm. "Oh, Frank, I need your help before you go. Can you please assist the driver with my luggage?"

"Sure. No problem."

Between him and the driver they got the two trunks and one carpetbag loaded onto the wagon.

Rachel turned toward her little brother. "I have to go now, Frank. Thank you for coming by to see me."

He wrapped her in his arms. "I wouldn't have missed it for the world and I have to go, too. Can't be late when you ride for the Pony Express."

She laughed. "No, I suppose not. I love you. Please be careful."

"I'm always careful." He released her. "Love you, Sis." He walked out the door.

"Hey, Mrs. Maitland, you comin'?"

"Yes, just let me lock the door." She took one last look at the house that had been her home for almost the last ten years. The worn-out carpet down the hallway and up the wide staircase, started out blue, but now was gray. The wallpaper below the chair rail bubbled and would soon begin to peel. The wood all over the house needed to be refinished.

So many tasks to accomplish, but Claude never seemed to find the time to get the workmen in to do the jobs. Now, she knew why. They were broke and living on credit. His lenders had come calling the day of his funeral, wanting their money. She managed to get them to give her until the end of the following month to sell everything and get them the money owed. Fifteen thousand dollars and change was all she got for everything. The things she didn't sell were what she brought to the marriage and her clothing. Her pearl necklace and ear bobs were from her grandmother. She also kept her diamond engagement ring. Those were hers, and she wasn't about to give them up to pay for Claude's gambling debts.

She locked the door, and with it closed off that part of her life forever. Then she turned to the freight wagon driver. "I'm ready, sir. Thank you for waiting."

"Yes, ma'am. Let me help you into the wagon. It's a long way up to the bench."

He lifted her by the waist to the first step.

She climbed the rest of the way up the wagon and onto the bench.

He hurried around the wagon and up next to her.

"Mr. Von Glinski, thank you for being available to help me."

"You're very welcome, Mrs. Maitland." He furrowed his bushy brows. "Lots of things can be said about your husband, but to me and mine, he was a good man. He gave me the down payment to buy my freight company. Helping you is a small way I can pay him back."

Surprised that anyone had anything good to say about Claude, she held back a tear. She wouldn't miss him, not really, but she'd grown up with him and he'd provided her with a life and security she'd never known before. He'd turned her into a lady, for that she was grateful. "That's so kind of you to say. Thank you. I needed to hear that he was a good man to someone."

Arriving at the stage depot, Rachel turned to pay Mr. Von Glinski and held out twenty-five dollars to him.

He shook his head and waved his hands in front of him. "I can't take your money."

"Please, take the money. Buy a treat for your family."

"Mrs. Maitland, you are too kind. Just like your husband."

Rachel smiled and shook the man's hand, then picked up her carpetbag and entered the stage depot where she went to the ticket window.

"I'd like a ticket to Carson City, in the Nevada Territory, please."

"That'll be one-hundred-ninety-six dollars and fifty-cents, please."

Rachel pulled the money out of her purse. Mr. Johnson, her intended, had sent her four-hundred-and-fifty dollars for travel expenses. At this rate, after buying some practical clothes for her new life on the frontier, she'd be lucky to have anything left when she reached Carson City.

The ticket agent took her money and handed her a book of tickets. "The meals at the stage stops are one-dollar. Just wanted you to be aware. If the ladies of the town are selling box lunches, that's the way to go. The stage stop food leaves a lot to be desired, other than it is filling. The trip will take approximately twenty-five days or more, so that's a lot of meals."

Twenty-five days! I've never taken a stagecoach anywhere before and it turns out this will be the longest trip I've ever taken...period. Claude had picked her up at her father's farm outside Kansas City in a surrey. He'd insisted she needn't bring anything with her that he would provide her with everything she needed or wanted.

"Thank you for the information. I appreciate it very much."

The little man tipped his hat. "Glad to be of service."

Rachel went outside and boarded the coach even though it was early. She might as well sit and get a good seat next to the window. She certainly didn't want to be stuck in the middle.

When she got to the coach three people were already inside, two men and one woman. They all had window seats on the unpadded benches. The poor woman looked like she was expecting. This trip would not be easy for her.

One of the men was quite overweight and sweating profusely. "I wish this thing would get going. I need a breeze." He blotted his forehead with a handkerchief.

Rachel took the last seat by a window. About ten minutes later, two ladies entered the coach and took the remaining middle seats.

The shotgun rider climbed up to the top of the stage where he and the driver sat. "All aboard, Zeke."

"Let's get this trip underway. Giddy up."

She heard the crack of a whip, and the coach began to move. Before she knew it, they were headed out of town. The seat was very hard, and her bum would be sore after just a few hours. She'd decided against wearing her hoops and had taken up the hem on all her skirts. However, they were still bulky, and it fought for room with the skirt of the woman next to her. Even sitting on the excess material didn't provide enough padding to the bench. She had a heavy wool sweater in her carpetbag. She'd get it out at the first stop and sit on it for some padding and, hopefully, more comfort.

The man across from her, in the brown suit, with brown hair and beard cleared his throat. "We'll be on this coach together for some time. I suggest we introduce ourselves. I'm Thaddeus Ridgeway. I'm a banker and will be opening a new bank in Carson City in the Nevada Territory. Is anyone else going that far?"

Rachel raised her hand. “I am. I’m Rachel Maitland. I’m a widow and a mail-order bride. My future husband lives in Carson City.”

Mr. Ridgeway tipped his hat. “Pleased to meet you Mrs. Maitland. Who is your intended husband? I might know him.”

“You as well, sir. Undoubtedly, you do. He is Elijah Johnson. I believe he is a miner.”

“Unfortunately, I have not made his acquaintance.”

The woman next to Mr. Ridgeway was small and timid looking. She looked like a strong wind could blow her away. Wearing a gray traveling suit, which did nothing for her complexion, she looked gaunt and pale. “I’m Temperance Sutton and that is my mother, Harriet Sutton.” She pointed at the woman sitting next to Rachel. “We are going to stay with my brother in Denver.”

“That’s right,” said Harriet who was the opposite of her daughter. She was quite stocky and wore a two-piece traveling suit. Her gray hair was done in the latest style, parted in the middle, and then gathered in a chignon at the back of her head.

Rachel would love to be able to style her hair that way…well except for the part in the middle. She thought it made her look too severe.

Harriet continued berating her daughter. “He has agreed to take us in and provide a proper education for Temperance.”

Rachel thought Mrs. Sutton was quite haughty and didn't believe, by the frown and sad eyes on Temperance, that she was very happy about the arrangement. She would have been a pretty girl if not so sad. With big blue eyes and hair the color of corn silk, she was quite attractive.

"We could have stayed." Temperance wrung her hands on her lap. "Gerald already said that he would allow you to live with us when we married."

"You are not marrying that…that…farmer." She raised a fist and then relaxed her hand enough to clasp the other on her lap. "I refuse to see you throw your life away on a piece of dirt."

Temperance leaned forward and held her hands palm up. "But Mama, Gerald and I love each other."

The coach hit a particularly deep hole in the road and although Rachel's bottom didn't move, wedged in next to each other as they were, her chest did and she rocked back and forth.

Mrs. Sutton lifted her chin and literally looked down her nose at her daughter. "Nonsense. Marriage has no room for love. You marry for status and protection."

Temperance slumped and dropped her hands into her lap. "Gerald could have provided us protection and I'd be happy. What is so wrong with that?"

"Hush girl." Harriet pointed her finger at her daughter. "We've been through this. I will not have you marrying him. That's the end of it."

As if to put an end to the conversation, a gust of wind sprayed dust into the carriage. Everyone was covered.

She watched a tear roll down the young woman's cheek. Rachel disagreed with the mother completely. She hoped very much to find love in her upcoming marriage. Though she hadn't loved Claude, she had respected and cared for him. At least until he died and she found out what he was doing with their money.

Next to Temperance sat the pregnant woman. "I'm Priscilla Clayton. My husband is stationed at Fort Laramie. I'm joining him there."

Rachel smiled at the girl, who couldn't have been more than about twenty. "When are you due, my dear?"

"Not for another month, but Gregory and I wanted to be together when the baby comes."

"Of course. That's one of the best things about babies…bringing together families." *If only I could have had a child with Claude.*

The girl smiled at Rachel. "How many children do you have Mrs. Maitland?"

I felt like someone had stabbed me in the chest at having to admit my failure as a woman. Barren. That's what Claude's doctor had said. "Alas, my husband and I were not able to have children."

Priscilla tilted her head. "I'm so sorry."

"Thank you. I hope you have a beautiful baby and enjoy him...or her…very much."

Priscilla put her hands over her stomach. "I'm sure we will."

The last to introduce himself was the sweaty man, with brown hair slicked down from a part in the middle. He wore a three-piece navy colored suit and sat across from Priscilla. "I'm Wilber Wooten and I sell women's ribbons, fripperies and such. Accessories that most women living in the country can't buy anywhere but from me."

Once they'd all introduced themselves, not much more was said.

For the next week Rachel spent her time at the window staring out, at least when the leather blind wasn't down to save them from the dust. She and the Sutton ladies rotated who sat by the window. They let Priscilla keep the window all the time due to her pregnancy.

When they'd reached the prairie or high desert as some people called it—the landscape rapidly changed. From tilled green fields filled with corn and beans and new shoots of autumn wheat to brown grass and rolling hills.

She knew from her reading that the great beasts she saw were buffalo. There were thousands of them. The stagecoach slowed as we passed a great herd. Once they were through, the driver cracked the whip and they were off again, galloping across the countryside. She saw more rabbits than she could imagine and the antelope were only outnumbered by the buffalo.

Rachel knew they followed a river called South Platte. Some days she could see it, some days she heard it when they stopped and sometimes she was sure they'd left the river behind only to have it show itself the next day. She supposed that was why it was called the high desert. The South Platte River was the only source of water she saw. No other rivers or lakes.

By the time she reached Denver, her bottom was completely numb.

In Denver they lost Priscilla, the Sutton's, and Mr. Wooten…all of them were off to different destinations. The stage she was on went through to Sacramento and right through Carson City. She and Mr. Ridgeway stayed on.

They acquired new passengers in Denver. A young couple who were obviously newlyweds. They held hands almost constantly and whispered together the entire trip. They left the coach in Salt Lake City. No more passengers got on in Salt Lake, so the ride was more comfortable for everyone.

The leather flaps that covered the windows of the coach were rolled up now to let the air in, at least for a while, until the dust got to be too much to tolerate.

Rachel was never so happy as she was to hear the shotgun rider yell down, "Next stop Carson City."

She couldn't wait to meet the man who would be her husband and secure her future.

She'd kept track of the dates. Today was September 13, 1861, and she would be getting married today. Hopefully, she'd find someplace she could clean up and change clothes, before the ceremony. She really didn't want to get married in the same clothes she'd been wearing for the last twenty-four days. A bath would be heavenly. Some of the stage stops were long enough for her to change clothes but there was little privacy. A bedroom behind the bar with no door was the most private place she encountered. She made do with washing her face, hands, neck, and chest above her corset.

Rachel still had about forty-five dollars, give or take, from the money Mr. Johnson sent her, fifty dollars left from the money remaining after all Claude's creditors had been paid and the four-hundred-fifty dollars from the sale of her ball gowns. With a total of five-hundred and forty-five dollars, she could afford a bath and a room in the hotel where she could change clothes and refresh herself after the long, long trip.

The stage stopped in front of the Carson City Hotel.

The driver, Zeke Smith, came around to her side of the coach. "May I help you down, Mrs. Maitland?"

"Yes, Mr. Smith, thank you."

"You've been a perfect passenger and I thank you

for that. You never complained, always had a smile for everyone. You've been the nicest lady we've had the pleasure of transporting in our coach."

Rachel smiled. "I simply think I don't know about someone's life and what would make them cranky. Sometimes a smile is all it takes to set them on a better day."

"You have a good life, Mrs. Maitland."

"I will, Mr. Smith. I will."

Rachel walked up the stairs to the boardwalk in front of the hotel. A tall, handsome man was leaning against the building with one booted foot on the wall. He pushed off the wall and walked toward her.

"Mrs. Rachel Maitland?"

"Yes, that's me. Are you Mr. Johnson?" Her heart began to pound. *I can't believe he's so much closer in age to me. I think I may be happier in this marriage.*

"No, I'm sorry to say that Elijah got cold feet and left town two weeks ago but he told me you were coming."

She sighed. *What will I do now? Perhaps I can find a café that will hire me as a cook. I guess I do know how to do that.* She noticed the star on his vest. "Marshal?"

"Egan, ma'am. Joshua Egan, and I have a proposition for you, Mrs. Maitland. If you'll come inside, we can discuss it over coffee in the hotel restaurant."

"A proposition?"

"Yes, ma'am. Follow me."

She bent to pick up her carpetbag.

"Here, let me take that."

What kind of proposition could the marshal have?

CHAPTER TWO

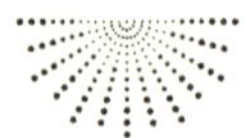

September 13, 1861

Rachel followed Marshal Egan into the restaurant. The smells coming from the kitchen made her mouth water and her stomach growl. *I hope he didn't hear that.*

The restaurant was lovely but small. Only about a dozen tables filled the space. Each table was covered in a white tablecloth with red roses embroidered around the edge. A pint-sized mason jar filled with wildflowers stood in the center. She didn't recognize the varieties but they were beautiful and appropriate for the setting. The single large window was covered with white lace curtains. The patrons could see out but it was harder to see in through the lace.

The walls were papered with vines and red roses that matched the ones on the tablecloth. The effect was charming.

They were seated at a table on the side of the room. The marshal sat with his back to the wall facing the rest of the room. His gaze scanned the room.

A thin, brown-haired woman with spectacles approached the table. "Hi. I'm Jane, your waitress. Can I get you something to drink?"

Joshua looked up at her. "My usual, Janie."

"Sure thing, Marshal. And you ma'am?"

"Coffee with cream and sugar, please."

"The sugar is there on the table, and I'll bring cream with the coffee." She bustled away.

The marshal…Joshua…smiled after the waitress. "I've known her since she was in grade school."

Well, that explains the familiarity between them. "That's nice."

"Yeah, she and her husband got married last year and I gave her away since her father left when she was just two."

"That's a very good thing you did." She looked down at her lap where she clasped her hands. "You said that Mr. Johnson got cold feet, but what am I to do now? Did he tell you why he was leaving? It had to be more than marriage to me."

The marshal's hands were clasped on the table. "I believe he was afraid of marriage in general, not just to you. If he'd seen you he'd never have left."

Her face heated. “That’s very kind of you to say.”

He shook his head once. “Nothing kind about it. You’re very attractive, Mrs. Maitland.”

“Rachel, please.”

“And I’m Joshua.”

She realized then that she was very hungry. Having refused to eat beans and bread one more time, she hadn’t eaten since breakfast the day before, if you can call more beans breakfast. “So tell me what you recommend here and then what your proposition is.”

“The stew is good, so is the chili. Steaks are always good. They have the best beef supplier and Sally Rogers, the owner, won’t share who it is.”

“I don’t blame her for that. If you all could get the same meat and prepare it at home, you wouldn’t come here.”

He chuckled. “You’re right about that.”

Jane returned for their order. The ticket clerk at the stage depot in St. Joseph was right about the food at the stagecoach stations. It was horrible and was extremely overpriced at a dollar per meal. She skipped more meals at the stations than she ate and bought the box lunches whenever possible. Even so Rachel was starving for some real food.

“I’ll have a steak, medium rare, with mashed potatoes and green beans.” Rachel’s mouth watered just saying the words out loud.

The marshal looked up at Jane. “Make that two.”

Rachel tilted her head at the marshal. "Now, your proposition."

Joshua clasped his hands on the table and frown lines creased his brow. "I want you to marry me. I have four children who need a mother. My wife died five months ago. I have a nine-year-old daughter, four-year-old twin boys, and a six-month-old baby girl."

A baby? Of course. "Yes. I'll do it." Rachel grinned. She was thrilled at the prospect of raising children. She couldn't have any of her own, so this was the best she could hope for. And marriage to a marshal meant security and safety, something she needed desperately.

The marshal's mouth dropped open. "You don't have to think about it?"

"No. I'm excited at the prospect of raising children. I guess I should tell you now." Her stomach twisted, but she knew she had to tell him her physical problem. She leaned forward and put her hand to the side of her mouth before whispering, "I'm barren. I can't have children. If you want to take back your proposal, I understand." She hoped he didn't rescind his offer, the thought of having to survive on the five-hundred and forty-five dollars she had until she could find a job and a place to live terrified her.

He furrowed his brows. "How can you be sure?"

"I was married to my husband, Claude, for nine years and never got pregnant."

"I don't suppose the fact it could be him ever occurred to you."

She sat back but continued to speak softly. "No. Claude was sure it was me." She paused. *What if it wasn't me? What if I can have children with Joshua*? "I do have one request before we marry."

The marshal cocked a brow. "What is that?"

"I want to get a room here, have a bath, and change into different clothes."

Though he was clean-shaven, he pulled his fingers down his chin as though he had a beard. "All right, I'll tell the reverend we'll have the wedding in about three hours. Does that give you enough time to refresh yourself?"

She smiled. The thought of being clean and wearing fresh clothes pleased her more than anything at the moment. "Plenty. As a matter of fact, why don't you make it two hours? I'll probably only need about an hour, but just in case, two will work fine." She closed her eyes for a moment picturing being in the bathtub with bubbles and a few drops of her lilac oil.

Jane brought their meals and Rachel dug in. The steak was cooked and seasoned to perfection. She'd never had better anywhere; even the fancy restaurants Claude preferred couldn't hold a candle to this meat.

Neither of them talked much.

"I'm so sorry your wife passed."

"Thank you."

"Was she ill?"

His mouth flattened into a straight line. "She was murdered during a stagecoach robbery."

Rachel covered her mouth with her hand. "Oh, my God. Have you caught those responsible?" *This town is much more dangerous than St. Joseph. Is Joshua the only law enforcement here? How does he manage to keep the peace and look for his wife's murderer?*

"No. But I will if it's the last thing I do. I was lucky Gertie wasn't with her. It was just supposed to be an overnight trip to see her sister in Desert Wells. She and her husband run the stage depot there. You probably met her when you stopped."

She nodded, "Probably. There was a very nice woman there who gave me her bedroom to clean up a bit." She didn't say more. It was obvious the subject was entirely too painful for him to continue.

They finished their meal.

"Well, let's get you that room and a bath ordered."

"I do appreciate it. The trip was very long."

After she got to her room and the bath had been delivered, she added her lilac scent and some bubble bath.

Rachel smiled and leaned back in the tub. She quickly leaned forward again. The scented water hurt the sores she'd gotten from wearing her corset for so long without changing it. She did her best to clean the wounds, but it hurt badly. Even worse, she couldn't do much to the ones on her sides and nothing to the ones on her back.

Finishing her bath much quicker than she expected, she opened her carpetbag and pulled out the only dress inside. The dress was what she had planned to wear when she married Elijah. It was made of pale green silk with pearl buttons down the bodice and on the cuffs. It was wrinkled but she hoped by wearing it for a while, some of the wrinkles would disappear.

The marshal seemed nice, and he was very handsome, but the icing on the cake was the children. She couldn't wait to meet them.

She worked the tangles out of her thick, wet hair and then put the red mass in a bun at the nape of her neck. Rachel wasn't good with her hair and did the simplest styles, after which she donned a matching hat.

She put on her grandmother's pearl necklace and ear bobs. With no mirror in the room, she couldn't judge how she looked, but she'd done the best she could do. She folded her dirty clothes and put them in the carpetbag.

There was a knock on the door. *That must be Joshua.*

She opened the door and Joshua stood on the other side. He'd also used the time to clean up. He wore a black suit with a gold brocade vest and a cravat tied in the latest style.

"You look very handsome, Mr. Egan."

"You are stunning, Mrs. Maitland. Shall we go get

married? I don't want to leave my kids alone any longer than necessary. Maggie is very good with the little ones and very responsible, but I don't want her to have to watch them too long."

"I completely understand and agree." She picked up her reticule then placed her hand in the crook of his elbow.

He covered her hand with his for a moment and then picked up her carpetbag.

They arrived at a modest home with a garden in the front. The path was through the center up to the front door.

She was surprised that Carson City was so much smaller than St. Joseph. Between the reverend's home and the hotel, they'd only passed a couple of shops. A dress shop which she might utilize if she couldn't sew new clothes for herself or the children.

Joshua turned to her. "It's Friday so the reverend is not at the church. He's agreed to perform the ceremony here at his home."

He knocked on the door.

A tall, thin woman answered. When she saw Joshua, she smiled.

The expression transformed her, making her beautiful instead of quite dour.

"Come in." She stepped back and allowed them to enter the home.

From the outside, except for the garden, the home looked very plain but inside, it was decorated and quite lovely. The sofa was blue brocade, and the two Queen Anne chairs on either end were a solid matching blue. A coffee table stood in front of the sofa and all three of them faced the rock fireplace. On the mantel were various knick-knacks and a large painting of the woman and a man she assumed was the reverend.

"Hi, Margaret. This is my fiancée, Mrs. Rachel Maitland. Rachel, this is Mrs. Peabody."

Rachel bobbed her head. "So nice to meet you, Mrs. Peabody."

"And you, my dear."

Joshua squeezed Rachel's hand just a bit. "Is Wayne ready for us?"

"Oh, yes, he's looking forward to it. Let me get him and Fred, who will be the second witness. I'll be right back." She headed to a door that Rachel guessed was the kitchen.

In a minute or so, two men entered. The older of the two had brown hair which was more gray than brown. He was tall and lean, like his wife, and was clean-shaven, like Joshua.

The younger man, who had to be the son, was as tall as his father and had the same brown hair but with no gray and sported a neatly trimmed beard.

The reverend came forward. "Joshua. So glad you came. I'm delighted to meet your fiancée. What is your name, my dear?"

"Rachel Maitland, sir. Pleased to meet you." She nodded her head.

Reverend Peabody took her hand and shook it. "As I am you. Shall we get started? Go stand in front of the fireplace, please."

The marshal led her to her spot to stand and then turned and faced the reverend.

The reverend pulled a small notebook and pencil from his pocket. "Very good. What are your middle names?"

"Mine is Anne," said Rachel.

"And mine is David," said Joshua.

Reverend Peabody wrote in the notebook and then put the pencil back in his pocket. "Good. Let us begin. Dearly beloved, we are gathered here in front of these witnesses and in the eyes of our Lord to join this man and this woman in holy matrimony. Do you, Joshua David Egan take this woman, Rachel Anne Maitland, as your lawful wedded wife, to have and to hold, in sickness and in health, for richer and for poorer, and to keep yourself only unto her for as long as you both shall live?"

"I do." Joshua's voice was strong and sure.

Rachel was very nervous, so much so she shook. Her dreams were about to come true. A husband and children. She'd never wanted money or riches of that kind. The riches she wanted were children, and she was becoming the richest woman in town as far as she was concerned.

"Do you, Rachel Anne Maitland, take this man Joshua David Egan as your lawful wedded husband, to have and to hold in sickness and in health, for richer and for poorer, to honor and obey him and keep yourself only unto him for as long as you both shall live?"

Rachel looked up at Joshua, the man who was granting her every wish. How could she ever repay him?

He gazed at her and smiled.

"I do." Her voice wavered just a bit but was still loud enough to be heard.

The reverend raised his gaze to them from the Bible he held. "Then by the power vested in me by the Lord God Almighty, the City of Carson City, and the Nevada Territory, I now pronounce you man and wife. You may kiss your bride."

Joshua turned Rachel to face him, took her face in his hands, and touched his lips to hers.

She expected just a quick peck, but he kissed her, really kissed her and she moved her hand to the top of her hat to keep it on, afraid even the pin wasn't enough.

He pulled back and rubbed her lower lip with his thumb. "You'll do, Mrs. Egan. You'll definitely do."

"Oh, my." Those were the only words she had enough mind to utter. He totally took her breath away. Claude never kissed her like that. *Oh, my.*

Joshua picked up her carpetbag with one hand and

took her hand with his other. "Shall we go, my dear? I have four little someones I want you to meet."

At the feel of his warm hand in hers, she relaxed. "Yes, I can't wait to meet them." She turned to the reverend. "Thank you so much, Reverend Peabody."

"You are very welcome, Mrs. Egan. I wish you a happy life."

"Thank you. I'm sure it will be."

Joshua reached into his pocket and pulled out a five-dollar gold piece. "For the church, Reverend."

I didn't think marshals made much money. What if I've married another man like Claude? No. I can't think like that. Joshua is not Claude. He is not like Claude. Please let this be true. Don't let him be anything like my dead husband.

The man took it and put it in his pocket. "Thank you, my boy. Take care now."

The marshal nodded, picked up her carpetbag and pulled Rachel out the door. Once there, he put her hand through the crook in his elbow. "Well, how does it feel to be married again?"

"I don't know…yet. You're nothing like Claude, especially with him being so much older than me. He was very set in his ways."

As they passed a woman in her twenties carrying a baby, she called out. "Hello, Joshua."

Joshua stopped and Rachel noticed they were in front of a butcher shop.

"Hello, Wilma." He tickled the baby under the

chin. "How are you? Little Chester here is growing like a weed."

The woman giggled. "He is. We've just started him on solid foods. He loves mashed potatoes. How are your children?"

"They're fine. I'd like you to meet my wife." He squeezed Rachel's hand just a bit. "We just got married." He didn't remove her hand from his arm, but set the carpetbag down and then waved his hand between the two women. "Rachel Egan this is Wilma Sinclair."

Rachel dipped her chin. "I'm pleased to meet you. How old is your son?"

Wilma smiled. "I'm pleased to meet you, too." She looked down and smiled at her baby. "He's six months. Gertie and Chester were born just a week apart."

"They're good. Thanks for asking. Speaking of my kids, we need to get home so Rachel can meet them. Take care, Wilma."

"I will. You, too. Again it was nice to meet you, Rachel. I'm sure we'll be seeing more of you."

Rachel dipped her head. "You as well."

The woman walked toward the mercantile, Rachel and Joshua had just passed.

"She seemed nice. I wonder why she didn't question us getting married?"

Joshua looked straight ahead. "Because she's too

polite. Wilma is a good woman. She was one of Marjorie's best friends."

Rachel frowned. "Oh…even more reason she didn't ask."

"Probably because Marjorie and I were having some problems. That's why she was on the stage to see her sister."

"You're lucky she didn't take Gertie with her, you would have lost them both."

He winced. "I wouldn't let her. She wasn't nursing, couldn't nurse our children, so Gertie was already taking a bottle."

"I see." She didn't really understand but sensed Joshua didn't want to discuss it further right now. Maybe when they were getting to know each other a little better, she could broach the subject again.

"Continue with your story about your husband."

"Well, dinner was at a certain time and woe to the wife who was late with the meal. That was me, our first few months of marriage. After he hit me a few times, I made sure to have it right at six o'clock and not a minute later."

Joshua stopped, his body stiffened, as he turned to face her. "He hit you?"

She stopped, too, and nodded. "Oh, yes. He told me that was how all husbands treated their wives."

He dropped her bag and took her by the shoulders but his grasp was gentle. "No, it is most certainly *not* how all husbands treat their wives. I will never hit you, Rachel. Never."

She looked up at him, into his chocolate brown eyes and saw the truth. Rachel lowered her gaze and stared at her hands, clasped in front of her. "I was a fool, wasn't I?"

His brows furrowed, and he cupped her cheek with a hand. "You were naïve. Taken in and lied to by a man who should have been protecting you. That kind of animal shouldn't even be called a man."

She leaned into his hand, the warmth easing her soul. "You're a good man Joshua Egan. I feel it in my bones."

He lifted her chin with a single knuckle underneath then lowered his mouth to hers and kissed her, a gentle kiss, a whisper against her lips. "I hope you always think of me in that way."

What an odd thing to say. "I'm sure I shall. You're already ten times the man Claude Maitland was. And I was married to him for nine years."

"You were a child and knew no better. Don't blame yourself. Nothing you did deserved his treatment of you." Joshua picked up her bag and took her hand again. "Come meet my children."

Rachel's stomach flipped over. "What if they hate me?"

CHAPTER THREE

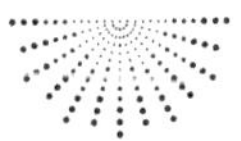

Rachel's heart pounded in her chest and her stomach turned over. "Really, what if they hate me?"

Joshua chuckled. "They won't hate you. Maggie will be the most difficult because she and her mother were very close. The boys will love you if you bake them cookies. Can you bake?"

"I'm a very good cook and I bake rather well, too. But if I couldn't, we could always get some here." She pointed at the bakery. The smell of fresh bread baking permeated the air and made her mouth water even though she wasn't hungry after the big meal she'd just had.

"But as it so happens, I love making cookies and that's something Maggie and the boys can help with if they want to. What about the baby?"

He raised his brows. "Gertie? She'll love you if

you just hold her and love her. You'll do very well with my children. I don't know why; I just know. Probably because you want children so much."

"You're right I do. I've always wanted children more than anything else. That's the only thing I truly regret. I could put up with anything if I had children to protect. I will with my life. I want you to know that even before I meet them."

They walked toward a large, white, single-story home, with pretty light blue shutters. Behind the home were a small chicken coop and a large barn.

Her eyebrows raised and her eyes widened before she turned her gaze back to him. "This is your home? I figured, with you being a marshal, the city would have provided something smaller."

Joshua smiled. "Oh, they did. It was too small, especially as we had more children. That home was only two bedrooms, and little ones, at that. Marjorie fell in love with this house and we could afford it, so I made sure it was ours."

"What do you keep in the barn?"

"A couple of horses, when they aren't at the marshal's office and a cow. We used to buy milk at the mercantile, but when Marjorie discovered she didn't have enough milk to nurse properly, we bought the cow."

"I haven't milked a cow in ten years. I don't know if I still can."

"You don't need to worry, Maggie milks her."

Suddenly the door opened and a little girl of about nine or ten ran outside.

She must be Maggie.

"Papa!" She slammed into him, her blonde braids flying, and wrapped her arms around his waist.

He placed his arms on her back and hugged her. "Maggie girl, I want you to meet someone. This is Rachel. She's my wife and your new mother. I want you to help her settle in. Can you do that for me?"

Maggie slowly looked up.

Rachel smiled and kept her hands clasped in front of her to hide their shaking. "I'm pleased to meet you, Maggie."

As she perused Rachel up and down, her eyes narrowed. "We don't need a new mother."

Maggie let go of her father and ran around the house toward the back.

Rachel put the back of a hand over her mouth to keep in the sob. Even though she knew this rejection was likely to be the child's reaction, Rachel's heart broke nonetheless.

Joshua put an arm around her shoulders. "It's all right. Don't let her response bother you. She'll come around."

Rachel stiffened her spine. "I know, and I'm trying not to let it hurt but—"

"Papa!"

Two little, blond boys rushed out the door and down the path, crashing into their father.

"How long has it been since they saw you?"

He chuckled as he tousled each boy's hair. "Three hours. This is always the welcome home I get and I love it."

"Tommy, Jeffrey, this is Rachel. She's your new mother."

"Can you make cookies?" asked the twin with the straight hair.

"Yes, I know several recipes for cookies." She answered the straight-haired twin she thought was Tommy. Rachel knelt down. "As a matter of fact, I bet you two can even help make the cookies."

Both of them widened their eyes. "We can?" asked Jeffrey, whose hair was slightly wavy.

Rachel nodded. "Yup, you sure can."

They looked at each other and both yelled, "Yay!"

Joshua gazed down at his boys. "Where is Gertie? Did you leave her alone?"

They shook their heads. "Maggie came in and took her out the back door."

Joshua rolled his eyes. "Excuse me. Can you watch the boys for me? I have to go get my daughters before Maggie gets too far away."

"Of course."

He ran in the direction of the church and was out of sight in a few moments.

She wondered if this happened often. How else would he know which way to go?

Rachel stood and gazed down at the boys. "Shall

we go inside? I'll see if we have the ingredients for making cookies. Would you like that?"

The boys both nodded.

"Why don't you show me where the kitchen is?"

Tommy linked a hand with her left. "Okay."

Jeffrey took her right hand. "We show you."

They took her into the house and to the kitchen. She didn't get much of a chance to look around, but she did see the living room had a lovely green brocade sofa and matching Queen Anne chairs, one on each end, all facing the fireplace. Bookshelves covered one wall and she made a mental note to remember to check out the books later.

Down the hall was a large kitchen. Along the wall to her right as they entered was a table, six chairs, and one highchair for Gertie. The pretty white tablecloth was patterned with festive red roses on green vines. Across the room were the cabinets, drawers, sink with a pump, and the icebox. On the wall between the table and the counters was a four-burner stove with green porcelain doors on the oven, firebox. and warming shelf. To the right of the stove was a door she guessed was the pantry.

Across the room from the stove, the wall had pegs for hats and a door to the backyard, which stood wide open.

Rachel closed the door. Then she looked in the drawers for an apron. She found one in the second drawer, just under the silverware drawer. She donned the garment over her silk dress and then looked for mixing bowls and cookie sheets.

She discovered Marjorie had been a very organized woman. The bowls and baking pans were in the places Rachel herself would have put them. She lit the stove and, while it heated, she gathered the ingredients.

The boys sat at the table watching her.

"When we help?" asked Tommy.

"Just as soon as I get the batter mixed and rolled out on the cutting board."

"K. You hear Jeffy. We gots to wait."

Rachel already loved these boys. They captured her heart when they accepted her without question except about making cookies.

She couldn't help but wonder at what a strange day she'd had so far. First no man to marry her, then marrying a stranger, a kiss like she'd never had before, rejection by one child and total acceptance by two others. *I wonder where Joshua went to find his daughters. And where is his office?*

Putting her thoughts behind her, she washed her hands, mixed the dough, and rolled it out on a cutting board which she took to the table.

She took a moment to check the oven. Holding her hand in it, she thought it needed a few more minutes to heat to the proper temperature. Finally, she could keep her hand in for only a minute or so, and that was hot enough.

"Okay boys, this is where you come in but first let's wash your hands." She held Tommy up so he could wash his hands in the sink under the pump.

"It cold."

"I know. I promise you won't have to wash in cold water again."

Then she held Jeffrey so he could wash his hands.

Then she handed each boy one of the cookie cutters she'd found in the drawer with the aprons. "You get to cut out the cookies. Let me show you how." Borrowing the cutter from Jeffrey, she pressed it into the dough and cut out a cookie. "Okay, now you do that."

The boys grinned at each other and then cut out cookies until the dough had to be rolled out again. She placed the cookies on the baking sheets and then rerolled the dough until there was only enough for one cookie, which she formed with her hands.

"Now I'll put these in the oven, and they'll be ready in about ten minutes. Do you want to go and play while I clean up our mess?"

"We help you," said Tommy.

Rachel touched his button nose. "Next time, you both can help me do the dishes, but I'll do them today and get the kitchen all tidy again."

The door behind her opened.

"Before your father and Maggie get back with the baby."

They had no dining room, so she wondered if

Joshua came into the kitchen for other than meals. Claude never came into the kitchen. They'd had a dining room so the kitchen was beneath him. Obviously, Joshua didn't feel that way. It pleased her that he would share a part of her world.

Joshua grinned. "Too late, we're back." He carried a blonde cherub with curls all over her head.

She was the cutest little thing. Gertie drew her like the flame on a candle. "I'm so glad you're back. Hi there, sweetheart. You're Gertie, aren't you? You're just the prettiest little baby I've ever seen." She tickled the baby under the chin and ran a clean knuckle down her soft cheek.

Gertie smiled and giggled.

"Do you want to hold her?"

She looked up at him. "I'd love to, but I have cookie dough all over my hands."

Joshua sniffed the air and grinned. "I wondered what that scent was. Molasses cookies if I'm not mistaken. And I rarely am. I'm a regular cookie connoisseur."

Maggie came inside and sat at the table, leaning back in a chair with her arms crossed over her chest. The look on her face, with lips in a straight line, eyes narrowed and brows furrowed, could only be described as mutinous.

Rachel washed her hands and then checked her pin watch she'd retrieved from her reticule. Ten minutes had passed. "Excuse me I have to remove the cookies from the oven." She took the hot pads she'd found and removed both baking sheets.

The scent of molasses filled the air.

The boys returned. "We have cookie now?" asked Tommy.

"We have to let them cool first." She put the cookie sheets end to end on the counter and as far away from the edge as she could get, just in case a child decided not to wait.

Joshua sat at the head of the table and placed Gertie in the highchair.

Rachel walked back to the table, took Gertie's hand in hers, and rubbed her thumb across the soft skin on the top of the baby's hand. "Where did you find them?" She didn't look at him but smiled at Gertie.

"I saw her at the reverend's house just before they closed the door. Needless to say, the Reverend and Mrs. Peabody were surprised to see two of my children on their doorstep."

Rachel ignored Maggie on purpose. First, because she didn't believe she'd get any answers out of the girl, and second, to punish bad behavior. "What did she think she would achieve at the reverend's home?"

He chuckled. "She asked them for sanctuary."

To keep from smiling, Rachel clamped her lips together. She'd have to keep an eye on Maggie. The girl was nothing if not resourceful.

"The cookies will be cool in a few minutes. Can the boys have a cookie and milk?"

Joshua grinned and nodded. "Only if their papa can, too."

"Of course." Rachel cocked an eyebrow and tilted her head toward Maggie.

Joshua sighed and turned toward his daughter. "Maggie has two choices. She can go to her room and think about what she did and how she will apologize to you…and to me, without a cookie now but she can have one after supper. Or she can sit here and feel sorry for herself and not get a cookie at all." He lifted a brow and waited.

Maggie stood and looked directly at Rachel. "I hate you. You've ruined everything. We don't need you. I can take care of my papa." She ran from the room.

"Well, I guess that's that. She certainly told me." She would not cry. Rachel swiped a tear from her cheek. She wouldn't…darn it.

Tommy and Jeffrey came over to her. Tommy spoke up. "We like you. You still our mama?"

Rachel knelt to be on their level. "I like you, too and I will always be your mama."

"Our mama left." Tommy, who seemed to be the spokesman for the twins, spoke with a catch in his voice.

"No come back," said Jeffrey.

Rachel knelt before the two boys. "Oh, my sweet

little men. Your mama didn't want to leave you but she didn't have a choice. If she'd been able, she would have stayed forever. She loved you both very much." Rachel wrapped them in her arms and hugged them tightly, while looking up at Joshua.

He mouthed, "Thank you."

She nodded, and then pulled back from the boys. "Are you ready for a cookie?"

Both twins jumped up and down.

"Yes!"

"Yay!"

Rachel stood, went to the counter, and placed the cooled cookies on a large dinner plate. Then lifted down the smaller salad plates and put a cookie in the center of each one. She poured the boys each a glass of milk. "Does Papa want milk, too, or is the coffee hot enough?"

"Milk, please. I'll share with Gertie."

Rachel set the plates and glasses in front of the kids and then in front of Joshua and herself. She sat on Joshua's right with Gertie on his left. "The boys helped make these cookies, didn't you two?"

They nodded and opened their mouths to answer, cheeks full of cookie.

She shook her finger. "Don't speak with your mouths full. Finish chewing and swallow first. Your father can wait that long." She looked down at the table to hide her smile.

Tommy showed Rachel that his mouth was empty and stuck out his tongue so she could see.

"Very good. Go ahead and tell your papa."

"We cut the cookies all by ourselves. Rachel give us cookie cutters, and we done it." He looked at his twin. "Huh, Jeffy?"

Jeffrey nodded vigorously.

Their father smiled at them. "That's very good. I'm proud of you, boys."

Rachel had been watching Gertie. The baby picked up the bit of cookie her father placed on the highchair tray and tried to put it in her mouth. Mostly, she mashed it in her hand and wore more of it than she ate.

Laughing, Rachel turned to Joshua. "Ah, Papa, take pity on her and put some of that in her mouth."

He looked over at Gertie, scraped the crumbled cookie off her hand, and placed it in her mouth.

Giving him a toothless grin, she smacked her lips for more.

He gave her a drink of milk and then another small bite.

Gertie grinned and slapped her hands on the tray.

The boys had finished their milk and cookies.

"Can we 'nother?" asked Tommy. "Pease."

Jeffrey nodded.

Rachel glanced at Joshua for guidance.

He shook his head.

She looked across the table at the boys. "Not right

now, but you can have another one after dinner." Rachel turned back toward Joshua. "Speaking of dinner, what would you like?"

"I bought a pork roast for today, but I haven't gotten it in the oven yet."

"Don't worry, I'll do it. Do you have a preference on what to accompany it?"

"Mashed potatoes and gravy, if you can make it. We haven't had gravy since before Marjorie was killed. I can't make it worth beans."

"Can me and Jeffy play in the back yard?" asked Tommy. "We pomise not to go out it."

Joshua nodded. "Sure, we'll call you when it's time to eat. Now remember, stay in the yard."

The boys nodded and ran out the back door.

Rachel stood and gathered the dishes. Then she got a wet washcloth and handed it to Joshua. "I thought you might need this."

"Thanks." He took the cloth and cleaned up Gertie.

She pushed away his hand and turned her head back and forth to get away from the washcloth.

He sighed. "Why do they always hate being washed?"

Rachel sat at the table with Gertie between her and Joshua. "Probably because the water was cold. I bet she loves her bath. I'll be keeping a bucket on the stove to have hot water all the time, so she won't mind it so much."

He tilted his head and gazed past her, a faraway look in his eyes. “That was something Marjorie always did, but I didn’t want Maggie to try putting the full bucket on the stove or having to get a chair to dip it out, so I stopped.”

Rachel tried not to feel anything, but she couldn’t stop herself wondering about the woman who had been his wife. “That was a good idea. Why don’t you tell me about Marjorie? It would probably do you good to talk about her, and I’d like to know the woman who created such a wonderful family.”

He was quiet for a long time.

She thought he might not answer.

Joshua spoke softly. “I met her when she was about sixteen and I was dumbstruck. She was so beautiful and so young, but I was determined, and I asked her father to court her. He looked me up and down then said, come back in six months, she’ll be seventeen then.

“So, I waited. The time seemed to take forever to pass. But six months to the day, I went back and asked again if I could court her. He laughed and said he didn’t think I’d be back, but he gave me his permission. We courted for nearly a year. On her eighteenth birthday, we got married, with his blessing. Maggie was born about ten months later.” He placed his forearms on the table and leaned on them. “What about you?”

Rachel gazed at the table. “Out of ten children,

I'm the third from the oldest. Though I rarely saw any of them besides Frank during my marriage. None of them managed to come for Claude's funeral, either. But I digress. We were very poor but, somehow or somewhere, Claude saw me and came to my father. He did actually ask to court me, but my father said I was too young. Then Claude, not to be deterred, asked to marry me if he gave my father five-hundred dollars. My father took it. I think I've told you the rest."

He shook his head. "You've not had an easy life. I hope we'll give you a better life than you've had."

She raised a hand and shook it back and forth. "You've already given me a better life. You've given me children, and I will always be beholden to you for that reason alone. I just wish I knew how to reach Maggie. After not getting a cookie, I don't think she'll ever like me. Though just being married to you might be enough to keep me from becoming her friend."

Joshua had no answers for me for dealing with Maggie. I guess I'll have to figure it out for myself. Maybe, since she wants to take care of her family I could let her help me cook the meals. I must consider this option.

CHAPTER FOUR

Joshua worked every day of the week. He and Ezra, his deputy, were the only law enforcement for Carson City. And though the town was small, there was still a need for the law. He took time off for church on Sunday and special events like one of his children's birthdays. So Rachel never knew for sure when he'd be home, but planned on around five o'clock.

Rachel began to prepare the roast for dinner. Taking the pork out of the icebox she put it in a deep roasting pan. She salted the outside of the roast and set it back in the icebox for an hour, then it would go into the oven. Rachel estimated a roast that size, about seven or eight pounds would take about two and a half hours to cook.

A knock sounded at the front door and she wiped

her hands on a dishtowel and picked up Gertie before answering the door. Two men stood there with her trunks.

"Gentlemen, come in. You arrived sooner than I expected." She stood back and held open the door.

They entered, and the tall, heavyset man spoke first. "Mr. Von Glinski wanted us to deliver your trunks first. Where do you want these, Mrs. Egan?"

"He is such a kind man. Follow me please, gentlemen." She took them down a long hallway to her and Joshua's room. She knew it was theirs because it was the largest and had plenty of space for her trunks. "You can put them against that wall." She pointed to the wall across from the plain wood bed, which was covered in a beautiful patchwork quilt.

She escorted the men to the front door. "Thank you, gentlemen. If you'll wait here, I'll get your tip."

"Thankee, ma'am," said the tall man.

Rachel got her reticule and gave each man two bits. "Would you like a cookie? Just baked today."

Both men nodded.

"Oh, yes, ma'am," said the tall man.

"Yes, please," said the short man.

She retrieved a plate with two cookies and gave each man one.

Gertie grinned at the men.

"She's a right cute baby," said the shorter man.

"Yes, ma'am, right cute indeed," said the tall man.

Rachel looked down at Gertie. "I have to agree." The men stepped out the door. "See you men again soon and thanks again," she called after them before shutting the door and locking it. *I can never be too cautious.*

Rachel was greeted with a foul odor. "Well, someone needs a clean diaper. Shall we see if we can find you one?"

She walked to the bedroom, next to the master bedroom. It had the crib and a full-size bed. Rachel laid Gertie in the crib. Even though reaching over the rails would make it harder for her to change the diaper, it was safer for Gertie than laying her on the bed would be. In the tallboy dresser, she found clean diapers, wool soakers, safety pins, and washcloths. On the bureau stood a pitcher of water and matching basin.

Rachel quickly cleaned Gertie, put on the new diaper and soaker, and a pretty, white dress.

"There we go. All fresh and clean." Picking up Gertie, she cuddled the baby. "What shall we do now? Are you crawling yet? Can we put you on a blanket on the floor without you getting away? Let's try it."

Rachel gazed around the room and didn't see any blankets. As she passed the living room, she saw the boys playing on the floor with wooden soldiers. She also saw a blanket on the back of the sofa and grabbed it.

"Will you boys be all right here by yourselves for a little while?"

Tommy looked up from his soldiering. "Yup. We fine." He put his head back down and studied his soldiers.

When she reached the kitchen, she placed Gertie in the highchair and spread the blanket on the floor. Then she put the baby on her tummy on the blanket and watched her to see if she'd be safe to turn her back on while she prepared dinner.

The first thing Gertie did was roll over and sit up.

"Well, look at you. Aren't you the clever one?"

"She just started doing that."

Rachel gazed at Maggie who stood in the doorway to the hall, with her arms crossed over her chest. "Really? Does she crawl yet?"

"No. She does what we call a turtle walk on her belly." Maggie demonstrated waving her arms like she was swimming.

"Sounds like I shouldn't put her on the floor if I intend to get any work done. Would you like to help me prepare dinner? I know you're used to doing it." She picked up the baby. "Or I could use your help watching Gertie."

The baby patted Rachel's face.

"What did you do with her when you were cooking? I don't want her to get burned or in other trouble."

Maggie shrugged. "Usually, I put her in her crib

with some toys. She can play for hours like that. Or I'd put her on the floor with the boys to watch her. They're really good with her."

"Thank you, Maggie. I appreciate your assistance." She put Gertie in the highchair and gave her a wooden spoon to play with. "Would you find the canned green beans and set them on the counter? Then we need to peel potatoes. How many do you think we'll need?"

"Mama taught me to make one potato per person. She figured that the twins wouldn't eat a whole potato, so Papa would have plenty."

Maybe I'm getting through to her.

Maggie tilted her head and looked at Rachel with narrowed eyes. "Don't think 'cause I'm helping you that I like you. I don't but I love my dad and if you make him happy, I'll get along with you."

Rachel clasped her hands in front of her. *I'm not reaching her and I don't know how to. I'm so unfit to be a mother.* "That's all I ask. I want to make your father, your siblings *and you* the best wife and mother I can be. I don't want to take your mother's place. I know I can't."

Maggie jutted out her chin. "That's right, you can't…you won't."

"Thank you for helping me, anyway."

The girl is quiet, like she's sizing me up.

"You're welcome." She went to the pantry, retrieved the green beans, and put them on the counter. Then she flounced out of the kitchen toward the living room.

Rachel's stomach was tied in knots. She'd thought she was making headway toward a relationship with Maggie but the child was only thinking of her father's and her family's welfare.

Thinking of the family, she heard the boys outside. She could see them out the kitchen window. They were playing soldiers using sticks for their guns. What an imagination these children had.

Glad to be in the kitchen after three weeks on the road, Rachel loved being able to cook for more than just her and Claude. That was the one thing she enjoyed about her marriage. When Claude entertained she got to cook all the offerings.

In the pantry, Rachel found the bin with potatoes in it. She pulled out six of the biggest ones. Claude had loved her mashed potatoes. She put lots of butter and milk in them and mashed them until they were creamy, but these needed to cook a little longer due to their size than the small ones she'd fixed for her and Claude.

She started them about forty-five minutes before the roast was done and when they were prepared she put them in the warming oven to keep the dish hot. She had to let the roast sit for ten minutes before it was cut. To protect the counter she put down a kitchen towel to set the hot roasting pan on.

Then she put the green beans in a pan to heat and

made gravy from the drippings in the bottom of the roasting pan after removing the roast to a large platter.

Most of the food was ready when Joshua walked through the back door right at five on the nose.

He sniffed the air. “Mmm. Something smells wonderful.”

Rachel was finishing drying the pots and pans as he came in. “I hope it is to your liking. I must tell you Maggie came in and helped me with dinner. She wants to make sure you are well taken care of. She’s a good girl, Joshua.”

“I know. I’m glad she’s coming around.”

Rachel laughed. “Oh, I wouldn’t say that. She made sure I knew she didn’t like me but she didn’t want you to suffer.”

Joshua sat at the table, shook his head, and then chuckled. “That’s my girl. As stubborn as her mother.” He straightened. “And the other kids? Were they good for you today?”

"And I’m sure she’s just as beautiful. You’ll have to beat the boys off with a stick when she gets older. She must take after her mother.” She grinned at her little insult and sat on his left.

He put his hand over his heart. “You wound me, madam. Couldn’t she take after me?”

She laughed. “You, with a face that only a mother could love? And the other kids were great. Gertie sat in her highchair and beat it with a wooden spoon I gave her and the boys played outside for a long time and then moved their play to the living room when I called them in."

Joshua threw back his head and laughed.

Rachel frowned a little. "Claude didn't like my sense of humor but I couldn't seem to keep it from our conversations. He hit me more than once because of it. I'm glad you appreciate it."

"The more I hear about *Claude*, the more I'm glad he's dead and can't hurt you anymore."

"I am, too, but then I feel guilty. A wife isn't supposed to be happy her husband is dead, now is she?" She frowned and looked away, ashamed of her feelings.

He placed a hand over hers where they rested on the table. "Every rule has exceptions and yours is a good reason to want him dead. No one in their right mind would begrudge you your feelings."

She withdrew her hands, but even as she did so, she missed his touch. "Thank you for saying that. Other than my youngest brother, who threatened to beat the living daylights out of Claude if he touched me again, no one has understood or cared what was happening to me. They didn't believe me because Claude never hit me where a mark or bruise would show."

"Tell me about your brother. Will I get to meet him? What about your other siblings?"

"Frank rides for The Pony Express. He might get

a run through Carson City and if he does, he'll stop for as long as he can. I'm hoping Carson City would be the end of his current ride and he could stay here for a while. But even if this was his final stop, he'd be back on a horse again headed back to St. Joseph almost immediately. He wouldn't even be able to see me. My other brothers and sisters all moved away as soon as they could, usually when they married. I haven't talked to them since I married."

Joshua smiled and squeezed her shoulder. "Well if things change, of course, he can stay here. He's your brother."

Rachel smiled. "Thank you so much. He's the only one I miss by coming here. He was just a child when I married and is only seventeen now. Do you have brothers and sisters?"

Joshua shook his head. "Only child, I'm afraid. My parents had me late in life, after years of trying. They finally gave up, and then I came along. They are both gone now." He looked down at the table.

Rachel placed a hand on his. "I'm so sorry. I know what it is to lose parents. And to lose a spouse."

Joshua's mouth formed a thin line and he gave her a quick nod of his head. "I'll get the gang that robbed that coach if it's the last thing I do."

He said it more to himself rather than her. She squeezed his hand. "I believe you will and if I can do anything to help you, I will."

"All I need from you is for you to take care of my children."

"Of course, I'll do that but if I can be of any other help I'll do that, too."

"Thank you for the offer, but all I want from you is a mother for my children. They are the most important people in my life and I trust you to care for my most precious babies."

Rachel smothered a smile. "I don't think Maggie would appreciate being called a baby."

He chuckled. "Probably not."

"Dinner is almost ready if you want to wash up."

Joshua stood. "I guess that would be a good thing to do and to make sure the kids are washed, too. The boys would eat with their hands caked in mud if I let them."

Rachel laughed. "Boys will be boys."

Maggie came in from the direction of the living room. "Do you want me to set the table?"

Rachel nodded. "That would be very nice. I'd appreciate it." She looked over at Joshua. He smiled like a proud papa that his daughter was being the helper he knew she could be.

The girl set the table for five.

When everything else was ready, Rachel placed the roast in front of Joshua. "Would you carve, please?"

He nodded. "My pleasure." He cut thin slices for

the boys and thicker slices for Rachel, Maggie, and himself.

Joshua dished up the boy's plates.

Since the bread available had not looked fresh, Rachel made biscuits.

Joshua piled his plate with mashed potatoes and topped them with the gravy and took a bite. "Mmm. This is great. Best gravy I've ever had."

Maggie's mouth formed a straight line. "What about the gravy Mama made? It was good."

Her father gazed over at her as she sat on the left side of Gertie. "Gravy was not your mother's forte but yes, it was good most of the time. Many times she had to throw it out because she got too much flour or too much grease or whatever. But this is perfect."

Maggie put a bite of mashed potatoes and gravy in her mouth. Her eyes widened and she took another.

Rachel took a bite of the green beans and swallowed. "The green beans are very good. I wouldn't have thought to season them with bacon. Did Marjorie can them herself? That's something I never learned to do, as Claude liked to have only tinned food from the grocers."

Joshua nodded. "She liked to can. We have many varieties of fruits and vegetables in the pantry that she put up."

As she learned more about her, Rachel was more impressed with the dead woman. She was also more intimidated. She could never live up to the memory of

Marjorie. Her stomach twisted a little at the thought. She took a deep breath and relaxed. She would simply do the best she could. "That's wonderful. It will save us a lot of money on groceries. Obviously you have a good butcher. This roast was trimmed just right. I'll go through your pantry and icebox and make a list of the things I think we need."

Joshua swallowed. "Yes, Klaus Bittner is very good at his profession. A list is a good idea. Marjorie never used one. She said she never knew what she might need until she went to the mercantile."

"Papa, we done. We get cookie now?" asked Tommy.

Rachel looked at the twin's plates and indeed they were empty. So was Maggie's.

Joshua took more mashed potatoes and proceeded to put some on Gertie's tray.

Gertie immediately took a handful of the potatoes and put them in her mouth. Or at least it was near her mouth. Most of it ended up on her face.

Rachel chuckled.

Joshua grinned. "She tries so hard to feed herself, so I keep giving her foods that are easy to eat with your hands since that," he pointed at Gertie, "is what happens to most of what I give her." He turned to the boys. "Yes, you may have a cookie now. You too, Maggie. I'm proud of you. Rachel tells me you've been very helpful today."

When he looked down at his baby daughter with

so much love, Rachel's eyes filled with tears. She so wished she could have children of her own. Another baby sister or brother for Gertie to play with and the other children to spoil would be nice.

What was the matter with her, wishing for something that will never happen? She swiped at her tears, determined she would love and enjoy these children she now had the pleasure of raising as her own.

But, oh, if dreams could come true.

CHAPTER FIVE

Billy really disliked using his fists on a man, but sometimes only he could get the information he needed. Using his fist, Billy hit the man again. “Where is it, Cowell? Where is the money?”

He’d come out to the desert so the man’s yells wouldn’t be heard and when he’d killed him, no one was likely to find the body.

His other four men sat around a campfire that was dying. Shorty, a short, wiry man with long, dirty brown hair. Red had red hair, hence his nickname. Curly was completely bald and rotund, wider around than two of the other men put together. And lastly Floyd, a big, burly man with blond hair and beard. His hair was so dirty now it looked brown.

Frank Cowell stared up at him from where he hung, being held by two of Billy’s cohorts. “You’ll never find it." He spit the blood out of his mouth. "It's gone, Billy. Gone." Cowell laughed and then choked and spit more blood.

Billy pummeled him some more. "We'll find it. I bet that sister of yours has it. Have no fear, Cowell, I'll treat her real good. Real good."

The man struggled between Red and Curly, where he hung by his elbows. "You leave my sister out of this. She's never done anything to you and doesn't know anything about the money."

"Ah, it looks like I hit a soft spot. That it Frank? You gotta soft spot for thet sister of yours. Real looker if I remember right."

"Leave her alone. She's got nothing—"

A shot rang out.

Frank Cowell stopped struggling and went limp. Not moving.

Billy holstered his pistol. "Had all I could take of his denials. Let's find out 'bout thet sister, pay her a little visit."

"Ah, boss," said Shorty. "She probably don't know nothin' and it be a two-week ride to St. Joseph."

Another shot rang out.

Billy moved his pistol aiming at each man. "Anybody else wanna complain?"

The men around the campfire shook their heads and put up their hands, shaking them in front of them.

"That's what I thought. Now mount up. As Shorty

there pointed out, it's a two-week ride. And bring those extra horses."

"What about Cowell and Shorty? We gonna just leave them?" asked Floyd.

"You wanna stay and bury 'em, Floyd?" Billy asked.

Floyd shook his head vigorously and backed up. "No, sir. Just askin'."

"Well, quit askin' stupid questions and git on yer horse."

Rachel needed to lock the doors and stood to do just that.

Joshua stood from his seat at the kitchen table and held out his hand to her. "It's time for bed."

She started toward the back door. "Let me lock up first."

He stopped her and tilted his head a little. "Rachel, you're perfectly safe."

Rachel took his hand and let him lead her out of the kitchen. "I always locked up before bed at home. I guess I'll have to get used to the fact I'm safe here."

A lamp burned on his nightstand, casting shadows on the walls.

The bedroom was chilly and she didn't want to undress. The house was only heated by the stove in the kitchen and the fireplace in the living room.

"It's cold in here. Have you thought about putting a small stove back here?"

Joshua shook his head. "It's not worth the trouble. We're not in the cold that long, only getting dressed or undressed. After that we are either in the kitchen or living room or in bed. Now, why don't you get undressed and get into bed?" He waggled his eyebrows. "I'll keep you warm."

She laughed. Then she realized she'd laughed more today than in the last year with Claude. The man was never home much, which had been fine with her. The less time she spent with him the better.

Rachel sobered. "I didn't want to ask about our finances in front of the children. Do you have an account at the mercantile or do I need cash to shop there?"

"I have an account, but I'd still like for you to moderate what you spend. Marshal's don't make that much money, but the city does give me a stipend just for food in addition to my salary."

She thought about the money she had left and realized she must give it to Joshua. *Are there more than just the butcher and the mercantile to shop at? Will I be able to find the goods I'm used to in order to provide good meals for Joshua and the children?*

"Joshua, you should know, I have money left from what Mr. Johnson sent as well as from the sale of Claude's house and furnishings and my dresses.

Together it's about five-hundred and forty-five dollars."

"That's good. We'll save it until it's needed, perhaps for new shoes and clothes for the kids. They grow out of them so fast, especially Gertie. Or maybe we'll buy some land and build a house. I won't always be a marshal, you know."

She chuckled. "Children always do, according to my sisters. And clothes, too. Building a house of our own would be wonderful."

Rachel got her reticule from the bureau where she'd set it earlier. "Here is the cash I was talking about. I still have some change, but I thought to keep that in case the children deserve a treat while we're shopping."

"That's fine." He stripped and got in bed. "Just set the money on the dresser"

Rachel was as nervous as she'd been on her wedding night with Claude, but then she'd been a virgin. Now, her virginity was long gone, but shaky fingers unbuttoned her dress. She'd done all she could to postpone the *event.*

Joshua watched her from the bed.

She finished removing her clothes and held her nightgown in front of her as she faced Joshua. "You should know I'm very nervous and I hope you'll take that into account when I ask you not to make love to me tonight."

He cocked up a brow. "Please continue."

Her stomach quivered and she felt her heart in her throat. She looked first at the floor then the window… anywhere but at Joshua. "The night Claude had his heart attack, he…we…well, we were having relations at the time. I could barely get his bulk off of me, and I believe the incident has left me afraid…unwilling...to make love."

"Rachel, put on your nightgown and then come here."

Rachel had always undressed in front of Claude. He liked to watch her. She turned her back to Joshua and donned her garment. It wasn't that she was ashamed of her body, but she'd known him for only a day, not at all long enough to feel comfortable with him. And she was terrified of making love. All she could think of was Claude's heavy body on top of her.

Joshua held out an arm.

She scooted next to him and then lay stiff as a board. Fear held her in its grip.

"Rachel, I'm a man, not an animal. I believe, once you get used to me and realize I'm not *Claude*—I can't even say the man's name without anger for the way he treated you. But, once you get to know me, learn I'm nothing like him and am not about to die on you, literally or figuratively, we can move forward with our relationship."

Her body relaxed. "You're not demanding your husbandly rights?"

"I don't care for an unwilling wife. I wish for you

to want me as much as I do you. I need that affection. To head us in that direction, I want to hold you, nothing more, just hold you, as we fall asleep. Will you allow me to do that?"

She nodded. "I think so."

"Good. Let's go to sleep. Sweet dreams."

"You, as well."

Rachel lay there for what seemed like hours. Finally, deciding his arm must be tired, she tried to roll away to her side of the bed.

He lowered his arm to the bed. "I see you're still awake."

"Yes, I am. I've been trying to figure out how to get to my own side of the bed so I can sleep."

"I'm crushed, madam, that you're unable to find slumber in my arms."

She giggled. "You're a crazy man."

"No, just a man with a beautiful wife who he wants to relax. Next time, and we will have a next time, just roll away or lift my arm from your body. I'll wake enough to let you move to your side."

"I will. But, for now, I will sleep over there." She scooted back to her side of the bed.

"Sleep well, Rachel."

"You, too, Joshua."

She turned over and wondered just what kind of man she married. Claude had been nice in the beginning, too. Will Joshua turn mean, like Claude did?

A week later, Rachel and Joshua still hadn't made love, but he held her every night, and she found she liked cuddling this way. Claude had never just held her. He would satisfy his need and then roll over and go to sleep.

She decided to get over her fear and let Joshua make love to her. That night she eschewed her nightgown, something Claude had insisted on. She had to be naked when she went to bed. She could get up after and put it on, but not in his presence. She came to bed and scooted into Joshua's arms as usual but then she put her leg over his.

"I'm ready for you to make love to me." She couldn't help but notice how his body was hard and muscular. Claude had been fat and flabby. She ran her hand up his chest and let the sparse curly hair wrap around her fingers. Rachel was fascinated by his body and couldn't help but touch him, learning every plane, every valley on his muscled abdomen.

He lifted his eyebrows and smiled. "Are you sure? I don't want you to feel as though you have to."

"I don't feel pressured. You've been very patient with me and I appreciate it. I truly am ready. Your body is amazing. I love to touch you."

"It's just a body. Nothing special."

She turned her gaze up to meet his. "You're wrong. You are very special. I've never felt a man's body like yours. Claude was my only experience with a man and he was not muscled anywhere. He was old and fat and flabby. I much prefer your body."

"Thank you. I'm glad." He turned over so he was above her. He kissed her gently at each temple. "Have I told you that you have the most amazing crystal blue eyes?"

She shook her head. "No, I don't believe you have."

"Well I've been negligent because you do and with your fiery hair you're a very beautiful woman. I see what Claude saw in you."

"Thank you and stop talking."

He chuckled. "Yes, ma'am."

Working down her body he kissed her everywhere. Then he pleasured her and she shattered into a million tiny sparkling pieces.

Breathing hard, she could barely speak. "Oh, my God. I've never felt like that before."

Joshua raised his eyebrows. "Claude never pleasured you…ever?"

She shook her head. "No. He just did the deed and then rolled off me."

"Well, I'm not that way. I want you to enjoy it when we make love as much as I do."

He kissed her, deeply, gently and thoroughly before he made love to her.

Afterward, she felt limp and complete as she'd never felt before.

"I never knew making love could be like that. Thank you for opening my eyes."

Joshua pulled her into his arms. "That's the way we'll always make love…well, one way. I have much to teach you, wife. And it will be *our* pleasure for you to learn. Now, let's go to sleep and may you have sweet dreams."

"Who can sleep after that? I feel…invigorated."

He chuckled. "Well, try. Morning comes quickly and the children do not let us sleep, as you've already discovered."

She couldn't believe what had just happened to her. Would he really make love to her like this all the time? Or would he become like Claude and roll over and go to sleep?

The children were up at the crack of dawn and instead of feeling invigorated, Rachel was now tired. Happy, but tired.

The first up was Gertie. She needed changing and her bottle.

Rachel slipped from bed and dressed quickly before checking on the baby. She found Gertie sitting up in her crib, sucking her thumb.

"Hello, sweetheart. Are you ready to get up? Let's get you changed first."

Rachel laid her down in the crib, stripped her and

washed her with soap and water. Then she put on a clean diaper, soaker, and little dress.

"You look so pretty. What do you say we put a bow in your hair today? Hmm?"

She brushed Gertie's hair with her soft baby brush and then found some ribbon in the top drawer of the tallboy dresser. She pulled out the pink ribbon and tied a bow in the curls on top of the baby's head.

"Oh, yes, you're gorgeous now."

Rachel heard boot steps behind her. She turned and saw Joshua enter the room.

"I'll say. My baby girl is all clean now, just the way Papa likes her."

"Do you want to feed her while I fix breakfast? I thought I heard Maggie stirring so she might have gathered the eggs. If not, I'll get them and then prepare breakfast. It was always my favorite meal and one I enjoyed preparing."

"I'd love to feed my little darlin'." He lifted Gertie from the crib and kissed her forehead.

Gertie squealed and smiled.

"Looks like someone is finding her voice and happy to see her papa."

Joshua kissed her on both cheeks. "Are you happy to see Papa, Gertie girl? Hmm? Or are you just happy to be rescued from your crib?"

Rachel laughed. "Probably some of both." Across the hall she glanced at the boys in the full bed they shared. Neither stirred, so she turned and headed out toward the kitchen.

Joshua followed with Gertie. “Right behind you.”

In the kitchen, Maggie was at the sink washing the eggs.

“Thank you, Maggie,” said Rachel, as she did every morning. “I appreciate your help more than you know.”

The girl shrugged.

Rachel saw the half-smile on Maggie’s face before she shrugged. It was almost like she forgot for a moment that she didn’t like Rachel. Now, Rachel smiled. Maggie was coming around.

Two little men ran into the room and hugged Rachel’s legs, as they had every day since she arrived.

“You still here,” cried Jeffrey.

“You not leave,” shouted Tommy.

She knelt in front of them and wrapped her arms around them. “I’m not going anywhere.”

“Pwomise?” asked Tommy.

“Yeah, pwomise?” asked Jeffrey.

Rachel hugged them close. Their words giving her a lump in her throat and making her blink fast to stop from crying. They needed her almost as much as she needed them. “Yes, I promise.” She looked over at Joshua. He sat at the table with Gertie on his lap and smiled.

Maggie turned, her hands fisted at her sides. “You shouldn’t otta make promises you can’t keep.”

"I keep my promises."

The girl's face was red and she frowned. "Mama said she'd never leave, too. But she did."

Joshua stared at his daughter. "Maggie, you know your mother didn't have any choice."

She turned to her father, tears in her eyes. "Why did she have to die? You're the marshal. You were supposed to keep her safe."

As he put Gertie in her highchair, Joshua's body stiffened. "I'll spend the rest of my life, if need be, to find and hang her killers. But I couldn't do anything from here. I wasn't the shotgun rider. My job, my responsibility is this city. I couldn't have stopped it. "

Maggie ran to her father and threw her arms around his neck. "I know, Papa, I'm sorry. I just miss her so much." She sobbed.

Rachel's eyes filled with tears and she put a fist to her mouth to keep from bawling. Her jealousy over a dead woman seemed so petty considering what this family had lost. She continued with breakfast because the task kept her busy and let Joshua and Maggie have some time to just love each other and grieve.

After breakfast, Joshua gave her a peck on the cheek and left for work.

He was only gone for about twenty minutes when he came in the back door.

Rachel stood at the sink where she scrubbed the skillets she'd used that morning.

"You're back quickly. Is something wrong?"

He came close. "The information I received from the bridal agency said your maiden name was Cowell. Is that correct?"

Something in his expression, maybe the narrowing of his eyes or the wrinkled forehead, sent shivers down her spine. "Yes. Why?"

"I just got word that a Frank Cowell was found dead in the desert about fifteen miles east of town. A member of the Granger gang was with him, also dead." He grabbed her arms and turned her to face him. "What was your brother doing with the Granger gang? I thought he rode for the Pony Express."

Tears rolled down her cheeks. "Oh, my God. Frank." Her chest ached and her breathing was tight, but she locked her eyes on him as the tears continued to flow. "He does…did…ride for the Pony Express and I don't know what he'd be doing with that gang member. I've never heard of the Granger gang." She pulled out of his arms. "Let me go. Don't ever accuse my brother of being a gang member because he wasn't." She swiped at her cheeks and turned back to the sink. Her heart broke. Never had she felt this low, this sad, this alone. When she had Frank, no matter where she was, he anchored her. She loved him more than anyone and now he was gone.

Joshua came up behind her. "I'm sorry, Rachel. The Granger gang is the one that robbed the stage-coach and killed Marjorie. I've been doing my best to find their whereabouts. I send out notices and wanted posters that I have printed down at the newspaper office.

"I was told by the deputy from Cold Springs, about one hundred miles east of here, that they were seen heading in the direction of St. Joseph. I have a feeling they are looking for you."

Still not looking at him, she braced on the edge of the sink. "Why would they want me?"

"Did Frank give you anything before you left?"

"No, he didn't even have time to drink the coffee I poured for him." She remembered he seemed so happy for her. Nothing about his demeanor said that he was in an outlaw gang. He'd been sitting on one of her trunks when she came back. Nothing was different about him.

Joshua turned her to face him, but gently this time, and then pulled her into his arms. "I'm sorry for thinking maybe you knew more than you said and for your loss. Please forgive me."

She wrapped her arms around his waist and nodded into his shirt while she cried. "I'm getting your shirt wet."

"That's okay. It'll dry."

She pulled away, sniffling, but the tears weren't flowing anymore. "I must finish the dishes and then write notes to my family to tell them Frank was murdered."

"I understand and I ask you not to give any

details. At this point I can't have the information I gave you to be public knowledge."

She nodded. "All right. I'll be discreet."

"Thank you. I need to get back to work. I'll see you at lunchtime." He gave her a quick kiss on the lips and then left.

What in the world was Frank doing with an outlaw gang?

CHAPTER SIX

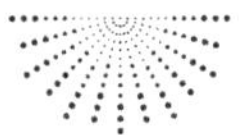

Rachel finished the dishes and then went to check on the kids. Maggie was watching them in the living room for Rachel while she did the dishes.

She walked into the living room only to find the furniture covered with blankets.

“What’s going on?”

Maggie looked up from the Queen Anne chair that was not covered with a blanket and smiled. “The boys wanted to build a fort and this is the result. Pretty good, don’t you think?”

Rachel put her hands on her hips and gazed at the chaos that was the living room and then smiled. “I think it’s a wonderful idea and a great fort they built. Where is Gertie? Did you put her in her crib or,” Rachel pointed at the fort of blankets. “Is she inside with the boys?”

"She's in her crib. It was time for her morning nap and she was yawning so I laid her down. She was asleep almost before she hit the mattress."

Rachel smiled and wrapped her arms around her waist. "Thank you. You are so good with your siblings. I'm really proud of you."

Maggie blushed. "Aren't all older brothers and sisters good to the younger ones?"

Rachel shook her head. "Oh, no. I'm one of ten children and my oldest brother and sister didn't want anything to do with us. I and my younger brothers and sisters were ignored or abused. They couldn't wait to leave home and we couldn't wait to see them leave."

Maggie's eyebrows lifted and her eyes widened. "Wow. Ten kids. That must have been fun though when they were gone. You could play with the other kids without the older ones being there."

Rachel laughed. "Well, it was much better. Until my father sold me to my deceased husband."

Maggie's eyes widened again. "Sold you? Oh, my gosh. How old were you?"

"I was sixteen and that is much too young. I was very naïve."

"Did Papa say so?"

"Your father told me how a husband should treat a wife. If you never think of anything else I've said, remember this, no man should ever lay a hand on you in anger."

The girl shivered. "I'll remember." Then she

looked down. “I’m sorry he treated you so badly and I’m sorry I was so hateful when you came.”

Rachel walked over to the girl and put her arms around her where she sat in one of the Queen Anne chairs. “You have every right to be angry with me but I’m not trying to take your mother’s place, I just want to find my own in this family. Do you understand that?”

The girl nodded. “I do understand and I’ll try to be nicer, but I’ll never forget my mama and I’ll never call you that name.”

Rachel squeezed Maggie’s shoulders. “That’s fine. I completely understand your preference and am happy for you to call me Rachel. Would you continue to keep an eye on the boys and an ear open for Gertie? I’m starting the laundry.”

“Sure and thank you. I never liked doing it.”

“I don’t think anyone does, but it must be done or we’ll all go around naked.”

Maggie giggled.

Rachel laughed and removed her arm from around Maggie’s shoulders. “You know, if you’d like, I could make you a new dress.”

The girl lifted her eyebrows. “You can sew a dress?”

Rachel clasped her hands in front of her. “Yes, I’m rather good at it. You can pick out the material when we go to the mercantile.”

Maggie smiled. “I’d like that.”

"Good." Rachel turned and headed for the kitchen.

The water was bubbling merrily. She brought in the laundry tubs and filled them with the appropriate level of water and added the soap shavings to the washtub. Then she gathered the clothes into a wicker basket starting with Gertie's. From there she walked to the boys' room, then Maggie's and lastly hers and Joshua's. She was glad to see that Maggie made up hers and the boys' beds.

Pretty quilts topped both of them. She assumed Marjorie made the quilts. They were all patchwork. Maggie's quilt was in tones of red and pink, the boys' were in shades of blue, and the one on Joshua's bed was blue and red.

She would do her and Maggie's dresses first, then Joshua's clothes, followed by the boys' clothes and lastly, Gertie's clothes and diapers. Rachel sighed. Laundry would be a long hard job.

By the time she'd gathered all the clothes, the soap was melted. For some reason, more clothes seemed to be dirty this week. Were they all changing garments more often?

Rachel smiled when she thought of the resolution of Maggie's dislike. She would and could never take Marjorie's place in the family, but if they could love her for herself, she'd be happy.

By lunchtime, she had just finished hanging Gertie's diapers and she still had to prepare lunch.

The roast beef would be good. She sliced it thin and put it on bread with butter and mayonnaise, then piled the sandwiches on a plate in the middle of the table.

She'd just finished setting the table when Joshua came in the back door.

"Roast beef sandwiches?"

"I've been doing laundry. This was all I had time to prepare. We have left over mashed potatoes I can heat up if you like."

"No, these are fine."

"What would you like to drink? Coffee, milk or water?"

"I'll have milk with the kids."

"I need to get them but you should come and see what they've done. They've built a fort in the living room. Your children are very imaginative."

He cocked an eyebrow. "What? This I got to see."

He followed her to the living room. When he saw the fort, his eyes widened.

Joshua whistled. "My goodness. This is creative."

"I didn't want them playing in the back yard since I was doing laundry today so they came up with this."

Maggie looked up from the chair. She was reading a picture book with Gertie.

"Hi, Papa."

"Hi there. How are my girls today?"

She grinned. "We're good. Gertie's been reading to me. She likes all the pictures."

"That's great. Your mama did the pictures and put

together that book when you were a baby. Did you know that?"

Maggie nodded. "I remember. You've told me before."

Joshua smiled. "Yeah, I probably have."

"She must have been very talented. I can't imagine doing something like that," said Rachel, just a little more jealous of Marjorie. Was there anything the woman couldn't do? "Anyway, I came to get you all for lunch. Tommy. Jeffrey. Come out of there."

The two little boys scrambled out from under the blankets. They ran to their father and each hugged one of Joshua's legs.

Tommy pointed to the blanket-covered furniture. "See our fort, Papa? Wanna pway wif us?"

"Yeah, come pway," echoed Jeffrey.

Their father bent and rubbed each of their backs. "I see your fort. You did a really good job, but now it's time to eat. Let's get washed up. Come with me."

The boys released him reluctantly. "Ah, okay." They ran to the kitchen.

Rachel followed them and prepared a basin of warm water so they could wash. Then she poured a glass of milk for each of them, including herself. She got a bottle for Gertie and prepared the milk.

"Lunch is served."

After the meal, Rachel cleared away the glasses and the large platter.

Joshua came up behind her and put his arms around her waist and his chin on her shoulder. "Do you still forgive me?"

She turned in his arms. *Claude never asked to be forgiven. He never thought he was wrong about anything. I don't know what to think about Joshua. Is it normal for a man to ask forgiveness?* "Yes. That is behind us and that's where I'd like it to stay."

"Agreed." He gave her a slow kiss on the lips and then released her. "I'll see you at dinner." He walked out the back door.

Maggie brought the plates and silverware to the sink. "Are you and Papa fighting?"

"No. We had a slight disagreement this morning, that's all. Nothing to worry about."

"Oh, I'm not worried. I imagine you'll leave, so it's just a matter of time." With those words, Maggie picked up Gertie from the highchair and went back into the living room.

I guess I'm not making the headway with Maggie that I thought I was.

Joshua walked back to the office. It wasn't far from the house, just a couple of blocks, but on the way there he couldn't shake the feeling Rachel knew more than she let on about her brother's death, but for now he would believe her. At least until he learned differently.

Frank was found more than ten miles off the Pony Express route in what is normally empty desert. It was a fluke that someone crossing in a wagon found them and reported it to the deputy in Cold Springs. What was Frank doing there if he wasn't part of the gang?

Mid-November 1861, Carson City, Nevada Territory

Billy Granger had found Rachel's former house in St. Joseph and conned her elderly, next-door neighbor to tell him where she was. Now, he was in Carson City and found the marshal's home. Wasn't that just the funniest thing? She'd married the same marshal whose wife he'd killed six months ago. He remembered her, he figured all the men did…before he'd killed her.

She kept saying her husband, Marshal Joshua Egan in Carson City, would never rest until he brought every one of them to justice or killed them himself. Billy'd heard enough of it before he finally put a bullet in her heart.

Now, he was taking the chance the marshal would capture him, but the risk was worth it for five-thousand dollars.

He walked up to the door just like anyone else would. Billy didn't check for the marshal. He'd already made sure the man was in his office.

Billy knocked on the white wood door.

A pretty red-haired woman answered.

"May I help you?"

Billy smiled his best smile, one that didn't show his brown and missing teeth. "Are you Rachel Maitland?"

"I'm Rachel Egan now." Her eyes widened as she tilted her head.

"Good. I'm Billy Smith. Can I come inside and talk to you? I knew Frank and just found out about his death."

She lifted her brows and smiled. "Certainly, Mr. Smith. Can I offer you a cup of coffee?" She turned to the blonde girl holding a baby. "Maggie, would you continue to watch the children while I talk to Mr. Smith, please?"

"Yes, ma'am," answered the girl.

Billy rested one hand on his gun belt and the other he kept at his side. "That would be great. I haven't had a good cup of coffee since I don't remember when."

Rachel led him through the house to the kitchen.

"Please have a seat." She went to the cupboard, got a cup, and filled it with hot coffee, before sitting opposite him.

Perfect. *She won't see I've drawn my gun until I put it on the table and it's too late.*

"So tell me how did you know Frank? Are you a Pony Express rider, too?"

Billy shook his head and pulled his gun from under the table so she could see it and know he was serious. "We did some business together. He was a good man. I was real sorry I had ta kill him."

The woman stared at the gun and paled. "Yo… you killed him?"

"Yeah and I've come to get what's mine. I want thet money he give you."

"I don't have any money. Frank didn't give me anything before I left for Carson City."

"Then he hid it somewhere." *Maybe he hid it in the St. Joseph house but I don't think so, not the way he was actin' when I mentioned his sister.* "And ya better find it ifin ya don't want those pretty little blondes in the other room to die." He glanced around checking for the marshal. Then he looked toward the living room to make sure none of the kids was listening. "It don't bother me killin' younguns. And you can't tell the marshal. If you do, the kids die. Do ya *understand*, Mrs. Egan? I'll be back in a few days and you'd better be givin' me thet cash."

She nodded and swallowed hard. "I understand."

Billy drank the coffee and got up to leave. "Real good coffee." He walked out the back door.

Rachel sat at the table, tears rolling down her cheeks. She didn't know if they were from fear or from grief over Frank. Coming face-to-face with his killer scared her. And the children. Why did she let a total stranger into the house with the children here? She's supposed to keep them safe and now she'd put them in danger. What if she couldn't find the money? Frank didn't give her anything, but maybe he put it in her trunks.

She'd been there two months and still hadn't unpacked except for her clothes. She was trying to give the family time to accept her before she put Marjorie's things away for Maggie.

Now, she didn't have a choice. She had to find that money. She had to protect the children.

Rachel swiped at her cheeks. This was no time for tears. Didn't her life with Claude teach her anything? He only beat her more if he caught her crying so she did it in the kitchen.

Joshua didn't stay out of the kitchen. They ate in the kitchen. Visited in the kitchen. Kissed in the kitchen. Did all sorts of things in the kitchen. She couldn't be crying when he came home and he could come at any time.

For now, she must start unpacking those trunks whether Maggie was ready for her to or not. She headed to the bedroom. Didn't even acknowledge the children as she passed by the living room. She didn't dare let them see her expression.

In her and Joshua's room stood the trunks. She looked in the empty one that had held her clothing. She'd unpacked and put the garments in the closet or in drawers in the bureau and tallboy dresser. Luckily, Joshua's clothes didn't take up much space, and she'd sold the dresses that would be inappropriate on the frontier, such as her dozen evening gowns. She did save one pale green silk that she'd gotten married in. She loved that dress and couldn't bear to part with it.

That was the one good thing about Claude. He made sure she was dressed appropriately. He didn't want to be ashamed of her when his *friends* came over. Those same *friends* who hadn't pretended to grieve for his loss. They didn't even come to his funeral. As a matter-of-fact, the only *mourners* were the bill collectors, who descended on her like buzzards when the service ended.

She looked inside the empty trunk and saw nothing untoward about the interior of the chest. Rachel ran her hand over the entire lining and found nothing. The lining was tight, maybe even glued down because it didn't move when she ran her hand over it. Since it was empty, it was time to relegate it to storage.

Joshua had storage in the barn.

She pulled the trunk by its handle down the hall, past the living room and into the kitchen. The dang thing was heavy. She stopped in the middle of the kitchen to catch her breath just as the back door opened and Joshua entered.

"You're home early. I'm sorry, I haven't started dinner yet."

"Don't worry about that. I'm not Claude, remember?" He jutted his chin toward the trunk. "Where are you going with that?"

"I do know you're not even the least bit like Claude and this trunk is going out to the barn. It's time to get those trunks out of the bedroom."

He hooked his thumbs in the front pockets of his pants. "I couldn't agree more, but I've been waiting until you were ready."

"If the trunks are gone, we'd have room for a couple of rocking chairs and a small table between them to hold a reading lamp. What do you think?"

"I like the idea, and I happen to have two rocking chairs in the barn. I took them out when Marjorie died. We used them to rock the babies to sleep. I'll get them when I take this to the barn." He lifted a brow. "Without dragging it through the yard."

Rachel smiled, to cover her fear, and clasped her hands in front of her chest. "That's wonderful. I'll get to the second trunk tomorrow. I must see to dinner now."

"You know we've used the same crib for all the children, even the boys. They were so small, and by the time they grew out of the crib it was time for a real bed. I guess Gertie will be the last one to use the crib."

She was stricken to her core. "I'm sorry I can't give you children more than you'll ever know." Rachel turned toward the stove to stir the stew for that night's dinner. She still had to make biscuits though she wasn't in the mood to cook, she had to maintain normalcy for appearance sake.

"Rachel, I'm sorry. I shouldn't have mentioned it. Believe me, I understand—"

She turned on him, her anger making her fierce. Her eyes narrowed, and she spoke just short of shouting. "No, you don't understand. You don't know what it's like to have your dreams shattered. To know you'll never have the one thing you've wanted all your life—children. I adore your children, but except for Gertie, they know they had another mother. Or, as Maggie would say, *our real mother*. No matter what I do, I can't win her over. I thought I was, but she stopped that notion completely today by telling me that I'll leave and it's just a matter of time. Is that what you believe, too?"

He put his arms around her waist and tried to give her a kiss.

She turned her head so he kissed her cheek.

Joshua sighed. "I don't believe you'll leave and I

don't want you to. The boys love you and so does Gertie. Maggie will come around, but she was closest to Marjorie and obviously misses her the most."

Her eyes filled with tears, but she wouldn't let them fall. "I know, but it is frustrating. No matter what I do, she still hates me. And don't say she doesn't. I think she helps me around the house and with the children to show you she's still taking care of the family. That she could do it without my help or my being here."

His chocolate brown eyes softened. "I know, but the fact is, I want you here. And she can prove she can take care of the family all she wants, that behavior won't change my mind about wanting you. And I do want you, Rachel. Never doubt that."

He gave her a long, deep kiss. "Do you believe me?"

She laid her head on his chest, though her muscles relaxed, her pulse raced. "I believe you." She looked up meeting his gaze. "I'll keep trying. Hopefully, we'll at least become friends."

"That's probably the best you can hope for."

"I know, but that doesn't mean I have to like it or that I'll quit trying for more." She sighed. "I love her, Joshua. I love all the kids. They are my dream come true."

"I know you do. I, too, hope Maggie will come around, but you need to be prepared for the possibility that the relationship you have now is all you'll ever get."

She let out a deep breath and nodded against his chest. *What if I never get through to her? Can I live like that for the rest of my life...can she?*

First I have to find that money. What if I can't?

CHAPTER SEVEN

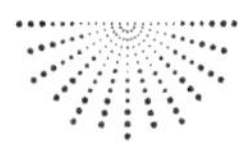

The next day Rachel was in the kitchen preparing lunch for the children.

A knock sounded at the back door.

She opened the back door and Billy Granger stood there grinning at her. His teeth were brown and he was missing his upper front two teeth. His evil smile sent chills down her spine.

Rachel stiffened her spine while her stomach tied itself in knots. She hadn't found the money. *The children were in the boys' room, safe.* She tried to close the door but he pushed it open.

His smile was gone now replaced by a snarl. "Now *Rachel* is that any way to treat the man who has yer youngun's lives in his hands?"

"What do you want?"

"What do ya think, *Rachel*? I want my money and I want it now."

"I didn't give you leave to call me by my first name. I'm Mrs. Egan to you and I haven't found the money yet. I have to empty the trunks slowly so I don't raise Joshua's suspicions. After all, you didn't want me to tell Joshua."

Billy narrowed his eyes. "You got 'til tomorra. If ya don't got it, one of those children will disappear until you do." He lifted a brow. "And if ya don't find it by the next day, I might just send ya a finger to let ya know I'm serious."

Her heart pounded in her chest. "I'll find it. Just give me more time. Please."

"Ya got my answer. I'll be back tomorra and ya better got that money." He turned and left.

As soon as he was gone, Rachel's eyes filled with tears, and her body shook all over. She had to tell Joshua, regardless of what he thought of Frank or of her. She couldn't risk the children's safety, but first she had to find that money. She ran to the bedroom and threw all the linens from the trunk onto the bed. *I should have just thrown the things from the trunk on the bed yesterday and let Joshua think what he would. This situation is entirely my fault.* Taking a deep breath, she ran her hands around the inside of the trunk. On the bottom she found a slit and a large envelope inside. She opened it and saw money. Lots of money. She placed the envelope in the bottom of the drawer she kept her under-things in. Then she took deep breaths and calmed herself. After she was ready, she went to the boy's room and found Maggie with Gertie and the boys.

"Maggie, I have to go talk to your father for a few minutes. Would you watch your brothers and sister for me?"

She rolled her eyes. "Sure. That's what I always do."

"I know and I appreciate you very much. You're a good girl and your father is very proud of you. Thank you for this."

Maggie narrowed her eyes. "Why are you being so nice to me?"

Rachel was taken aback. "I always try to be nice to you. Why would you think I'm not?"

"You didn't put curtains in my room or give me new sheets either."

"Honey, I didn't think you'd want them. If you do, I'd be very happy to give them to you."

"We went in your room and felt the sheets you put on your bed, didn't we Gertie?" She smiled down at the baby. "They're really soft, and I'd like some, too. And the curtains. Mine are old, and I want new ones."

Rachel smiled. "I'll give them to you as soon as I get back from seeing your father. I want you to lock the doors and don't let anyone in. It's important for your safety. Okay?"

She frowned but nodded. "I'll lock the door to the living room on my way to the kitchen and then lock that door after you."

"Good. I'll knock twice when I return."

"Okay."

Rachel walked to her bedroom and grabbed her coat, hat, and gloves. She stopped at the boys' room. "Okay, I'm ready. Shall we?"

"I'm following you."

Rachel nodded and watched Maggie's hand shake as she locked the living room door.

Unable to tell her what was happening and why they wouldn't be safe now, she couldn't do anything about her daughter's fear. When she and Maggie got to the kitchen Rachel turned her. "I shouldn't be too long. We can change your bed when I return." She had to try to keep from panicking the girl. Rachel was panicked enough for the both of them.

Maggie looked down at the baby. "Gertie and I will strip my bed while you're gone."

"Thank you. That would be very helpful." Rachel walked out the door and hurried to the marshal's office.

When she arrived at the small brick building, she took several deep breaths before going inside where she saw two desks. Only Joshua was there, at his desk, looking through wanted posters. A single wooden chair stood in front of his desk. A pot-bellied stove was in the corner and had a coffee pot on top.

Joshua looked up and smiled. "To what do I owe the pleasure of your company?"

Rachel wrung her hands. "You won't think it's a pleasure when I tell you why I'm here."

"Sit down and talk to me. What's wrong?"

She sat on the edge of the chair, keeping her hands clasped to stop their shaking. "Well, there is no easy way to say this except right out. Billy Granger is in town. He came to the house yesterday and said that Frank had something of his. Money. Five-thousand dollars, and that Frank gave it to me. But he didn't. I didn't know what Billy was talking about. But I went through my trunk and found an envelope with money in it."

"Five-thousand dollars? He must have robbed that payroll stage for the Comstock Lode last month. Why would he think Frank had it if he wasn't part of the gang?"

"I don't know." She fisted her hands. "I just know Frank was an honest man. Billy came again today and threatened to make one of the children disappear if I don't give him the money tomorrow."

The lump in her throat made it hard to speak. "I'm so sorry I didn't tell you right away but you'd already accused me of knowing Frank was part of his gang and I thought if you knew this, you'd be even more convinced. He was not. I'd never heard of Billy Granger before last week."

Joshua sat quietly but with his mouth turned down and his expression thunderous.

His eyes narrowed as she talked and now they accused her without him making a sound.

Finally he spoke, though very softly. "As soon as you saw him, you should have told me. I might have been able to arrest him. What did you plan on doing? Just giving him the money? After he murdered your brother and *my wife*?"

She looked down at her hands, clasped in her lap so he wouldn't see them continue to shake. "Yes. I was. I know it was wrong of me, but I just wanted him to go away. To leave us in peace." *How could I have been so naïve as to think giving Billy the money was the right thing to do? I was so stupid.* Her stomach clenched, and she thought she might vomit. She'd put his most precious things in danger. The children. *Why doesn't he yell at me?* "I'm sorry, Joshua. Sorrier than you can imagine. You can do with me as you please after this is over. I won't fight it."

He didn't look at her. "I'll decide what to do with *you* later. For now, I need to figure out a way to arrest Granger."

Rachel stood and headed to the door.

Joshua opened the door and held it for her.

Tears filled her eyes. He would divorce her over this situation and she couldn't blame him. What marshal wants a wife who would allow a criminal to get away?

When she and Joshua arrived home, he tried to open the kitchen door.

"Wait. I had Maggie lock the doors. I told her I'd knock twice when I returned." She stepped forward and knocked. "Maggie, it's us. Please open the door."

She heard Gertie crying and her heart hurt because she couldn't do anything about it. Joshua likely wouldn't allow her near his children again.

Maggie opened the door and ran into her father's arms.

"I've been so scared since Rachel made me lock the doors. We never had to lock them before she came." Her gaze shot daggers at Rachel.

Rachel hurried past her, following the sound of Gertie's cries. She found the baby sitting up in her crib, her face wet with tears.

When she saw Rachel, she held up her arms.

Hurrying to the crib, Rachel picked up the baby and found her wet clear through. "Oh, sweet darlin'. Let's get you in some dry clothes. Shall we? Hmm?"

Joshua passed by. "She can wait. Come with me."

Rachel turned on him. "You can be as angry with me as you want, but you will not take it out on your children. She's miserable and needs changing and loving. The envelope is in the second drawer of the tallboy dresser." She went back to caring for Gertie, getting her in a clean, dry diaper and clothes. When the baby's clothes had been changed, Rachel picked her up, kissed her button nose, and turned with her in her arms. Joshua hadn't moved. She passed him with the baby in her arms and led the way to the bedroom next door. Holding Gertie with one arm, she threw open the drawer. "There." She tossed the envelope on the bed. "I didn't count it but I'm assuming it's the five-thousand dollars he's looking for."

Joshua was quiet for a moment and simply stood behind her. "Rachel, I'm sorry. You're right, the children come first, and Gertie needed you. I know that now."

She didn't respond, instead grabbed some of her linens and threw them in the trunk.

Finally, after the last of the linens were in the trunk, she pointed to the envelope. "You can count it. You don't need me." She turned to walk past him.

He grabbed her arm. "You're staying."

Rachel gave a single nod of her head.

He released her and picked up the envelope from the bed. Joshua removed the money and counted it.

She silently counted it with him. Rachel had never seen so much money but Billy could have had it all if he left her alone and not threatened the children. Rachel wasn't proud of her actions and had no excuse for them. She'd never felt so miserable and full of guilt in her life. She should have told Joshua right away, but hindsight is always perfect.

He looked at her, his eyes a cold, hard brown.

"This is what we'll do. When Granger comes back tomorrow, you'll give him the packet. The money will be bundled tight so that he will see the real money and not the paper we'll put in with it."

"As you wish."

He looked at her, his eyes narrowed and his jaw clenched. "What I wish is that you had trusted me. But you didn't and now we have a dangerous mess."

She kept her back straight and her chin up. Though she deserved his wrath, she would not let him know how deeply his words cut her. "I know, and I said I was sorry. I don't know what else you want me to do. I'll sleep on the sofa until you decide to divorce me. I understand why you will, and I'll do whatever you tell me to do."

He lifted a brow. "Who said anything about divorce? I don't plan on divorcing you." Joshua ran a hand around the back of his neck. "We'll work this problem out, but I don't deny that I'm sorely disappointed and angry."

She nodded. "You have every right to be. Should I start cutting paper for the packet?"

"No. You go about your regular chores. I'll have Ezra do the cutting duty. He needs something to do, anyway."

"Fine. I promised Maggie curtains and sheets for her bedroom. I need to ask her what she wants. I'll be right back." As soon as she turned away, she could no longer hold back her tears and they ran freely down her cheeks. She stopped outside the living room and swiped at her cheeks. Gertie patted her face. Rachel thought she must feel the sorrow her mother felt.

Joshua passed by her, turned and wrapped her in his embrace. "I promise we'll be okay. Trust me on this, even if you can't trust me on anything else."

Her body stiff, she nodded against his chest, afraid if she relaxed she'd bawl onto his shirt.

He released her, gave her a peck on the cheek, and headed to the back door. She followed and locked the door after him. Then turned around and headed to the living room.

When she looked in, the girl was reading to Tommy and Jeffrey, one on each side of her apparently enthralled by the story.

"Maggie, do you want to come choose your curtains and sheets?"

"Yes, please." She stood. "You two can look at the pictures if you want while I'm gone."

Gertie yawned and Rachel stopped at her room and laid her in the crib. She sang to her until she was asleep and then walked to her bedroom next door. Picking up some pretty floral curtains, a solid blue set and a green striped set, she laid them out on the bed.

Maggie walked to the bed and felt the floral material and the blue.

The green set apparently didn't appeal to her.

"I'll take the one with the flowers."

Rachel held up the rose-covered curtains. "Those

are pretty. I'll get them ironed and hung today along with the sheets for your bed. Do you have a preference of those?"

"I'd like the pink ones, please. They kind of match the curtains, and I like pink."

Fighting to act normal, her chest was tight and her throat ached like she'd been yelling for hours. "Good choice. I'll try to get those ironed today, too."

Maggie tilted her head and furrowed her brows. "Why are you and Papa fighting?"

Rachel took a deep breath to calm herself before she spoke. "Sometimes parents fight but we'll work it out. Nothing for you to be concerned over."

She shrugged. "I just wondered if I'd get to keep the curtains if you leave."

For a moment, Rachel closed her eyes and then nodded. "Whatever happens, the curtains are yours to keep as are the sheets."

"Thank you."

She watched as Maggie walked from the room

Well, at least I made someone happy today. The sooner I'm gone the happier she'll be.

CHAPTER EIGHT

Dinner was a silent affair between Joshua and Rachel. She knew he was still angry and couldn't blame him. This was no little matter. She'd put the children's lives in danger after promising she'd protect them.

Maggie was so talkative that their silence didn't really matter. They couldn't have gotten in a word edgewise, anyway.

After the dishes were done, the kitchen cleaned and the children put to bed, Rachel had run out of reasons not to go to bed.

She entered the room and found Joshua already in bed, propped up by the headboard and pillows, reading a book. She donned her nightgown from the bottom drawer.

"No nightgown."

"I figured you wouldn't want anything to do with me."

He sighed, closed the book, and set it on the nightstand. "Rachel. We are bound to have disagreements…arguments…fights, whatever you want to call them, during our marriage. I'm not Claude. I want you to have opinions and not just agree with me. Though, in this case, you should have come to me. I understand your need to keep the peace and make bad things go away, but this man murdered both of our loved ones. How could you even think of giving him that money?"

Her knees shook and her stomach clenched. "I just wanted him to go away. That's all. I wanted to have him leave us alone and all I did was make things worse." Tears flowed down her cheeks. "I'm sorry. I know you're disappointed in me."

He got out of bed naked and walked to her, enveloping her in his arms. "Hush, now. We'll be all right."

She latched on to him like he was her life preserver in a stormy sea.

He kissed the top of her head and then raised her chin until she looked at him. Then he kissed her eyes and her cheeks and lastly, her lips.

The kiss wasn't carnal, but deep enough to touch her very soul.

I love him. He's not Claude, though I keep expecting him to be. Every time he proves he's not violent like my late husband was, I fall more in love. Is that all I needed…for someone to be kind to me? Is that why I love him?

"You can take that infernal gown off now."

She pulled it over her head and left it on the floor where it landed.

Joshua picked her up in his arms and carried her to bed, where he laid her in the middle. He lay next to her and stretched his arm behind her, bringing her close.

"I realize that part of this calamity is my fault. I accused Frank of being part of Billy's gang and that blame was wrong of me. It made you distrust me, and for that I'm sorry, too." He ran the fingers of his free hand along her neck and down to her belly where he stopped. "Did you realize that you've not had your menses since we married?"

"I know but it must be because of the change, stress related to marriage or—"

"Or you could be pregnant."

She shook her head. "That's impossible. I was married to Claude for nine years and never missed a cycle. Not once. He beat me each month my menses came because I didn't give him a son."

Rachel felt Joshua tense.

His jaw clenched and he spoke through his teeth. "I'm tired of hearing what Claude did or didn't do. The man was an animal and you need to leave that part of your past in the past." He turned her head with a finger to her jaw. "Don't you agree?"

She nodded, glad to leave that part of her life behind her.

"Say it, so I know you really mean it."

Rachel took a deep breath and whispered, "I agree to leave the past in the past."

He chuckled. "Maybe next time you'll say it with some conviction. It will take time to undo the damage that bas—"

She lifted a hand and put two fingers over his lips. "Don't curse. It doesn't become you."

He hugged her closer. "Now, tomorrow you'll do exactly as I tell you. Do not deviate from the plan. No matter what. Okay?"

She nodded against his chest. "I will not deviate from your plan. What if he discovers the money is only paper?"

"We'll arrest him before he can find out."

Rachel leaned up, with an arm resting on his chest, until she was eye level. "What if—"

He rubbed her back. "Follow the plan. Give him the packet and we'll take it from there. I've decided I'll be in the living room, listening and will arrest him as soon as he takes the money. Understand?"

She stretched forward and kissed him. "Yes. I'll do as you say."

"Good. Now," he rolled her to her back and came over her. "I need to make love to you." He kissed her, a whisper touch of his lips to hers before he claimed her completely.

The next morning Rachel prepared breakfast, washed the dishes, and started dusting. Anything to keep busy. Billy Granger was supposed to come and get the money. She would do exactly what Joshua wanted her to do. Give him the money and then step back so Joshua would have a clean line of sight.

Rachel tried to eat breakfast but vomited almost immediately. She was simply too nervous to eat.

"Rachel's sick," said Tommy.

"Yup," said Jeffrey.

"Papa?" asked Maggie. "Is she okay?"

Joshua got a wet washcloth and brought it to her. "Are you all right?"

She nodded and wiped her mouth. "I think so. I can't stand the thought of food right now."

He turned to his children who were still at the table. "She'll be fine. Now finish your breakfast." Joshua looked at Rachel, cocked a brow, and wrinkled his forehead. "Has this happened before?"

Rachel shrugged. "Yesterday but again I think I was just nervous."

"When this arrest is over, you'll go see Doc Goad. I want to make sure you're not sick."

"I'm not sick." *What if Joshua's right? What if I am pregnant? Could something that good happen to me?*

"Humor me."

She rolled her eyes. "Fine. I'll see the doctor."

He gave her a kiss on the forehead. "Thank you."

Joshua then went to work as usual, in case Billy was watching.

Rachel checked her pin watch again. Only thirty minutes had passed. When is he going to get here? When is Joshua coming back? Her stomach roiled. What if Billy comes before Joshua?

She went into the living room and watched the kids play. Maggie was trying to teach the boys to play jacks. They kept losing the ball under the furniture.

Maggie laughed and they started the game over.

Rachel chuckled. She was happy to see the three of them playing together. When she was Maggie's age, all her younger siblings did was make her crazy. All except Frank. Maggie and Gertie were almost the same years apart as Rachel and Frank had been. She doted on Frank, practically raised him until he was seven. Then Claude took her away. *Stop. I will not think of Claude.*

"Maggie, where's Gertie?"

Maggie looked up from the game. "In her crib. It was naptime for her. She kept yawning and falling asleep in my arms, so I put her to bed."

"Good. That's good. Thank you."

Rachel walked back to the kitchen and prepared lunch. Though she wasn't hungry, she had children and a husband who were. She'd made beef barley soup yesterday and it would be especially good today having sat overnight. There were still biscuits from this morning and that would have to do.

Joshua came home and used the back door as he usually did. Lunch went off without a hitch, but Rachel still didn't eat. She didn't want to throw up again.

After the children left for the boy's room to play and for Maggie to diaper Gertie, Joshua sat at the table, his hands wrapped around his coffee cup.

Rachel could tell by the way he looked into the coffee and leaned on the table that he was troubled about what was to come.

He looked up at her. "I have to go back to the jail. I'll come around the back way, so Billy won't see me and come in the back door."

She sat on his right and placed a hand on his arm before shaking her head. "You'd be better off coming in the bedroom window. Billy has used both of them and will surely have both doors watched. I would and I'm not a criminal with a gang to do my bidding."

Joshua thought for a moment and then nodded. "That's a good idea. Leave it open for me."

Rachel wrung her hands and paced the kitchen. "Of course. I wish we could send the children to the reverend until this is over, but I'm afraid they'd be in more danger there. The reverend has no way to protect them."

"I could lock them in jail, but I'm not willing to traumatize them, which it would since I can't tell them what the reason is. We'll keep them here with us."

"Besides, putting them in the jail or taking them to the reverend's house would send a signal to Billy that something wasn't right."

Joshua released a deep breath. "That's true and we want him to take the bait. The children will stay here."

"I won't let anything happen to them."

He stood.

She followed suit.

Joshua kissed her on the cheek. "I expect nothing less." He turned and left through the back door.

She'd tested his caring for her to the maximum, and if it happened again, he more than likely wouldn't be so forgiving. Rachel would make sure nothing like this ever happened again.

Standing at the sink looking out the window, she saw Billy Granger saunter toward the house. She began to shake. *Stop it. Just do what Joshua said.*

A knock sounded on the back door.

Rachel took a deep breath and let it out slowly to calm her racing pulse before she opened the door.

"Well, Marshal Egan's wife. You better got what I

come for or you know what will happen." Billy pointed his pistol at her as he came into the house.

Rachel frowned and ground out, "You will leave the children alone. I found your money. Frank slit open the lining of the bottom in one of my trunks."

Billy grinned.

She shivered. With his brown and broken teeth she'd never seen such an evil-looking man.

"Well, don't just stand there," he snarled, holding out his left hand. "Give it to me."

Rachel went to the pantry, trying to give Joshua time to get in place, and slowly brought the packet back to Billy. She held the money at her waist for a moment then shoved it at him. "Here. Take your blood money and go." She couldn't get against the wall so she backed up to the sink.

Billy grabbed the envelope, opened it, smiled, and closed it again. "That's a smart thing ya did, *Rachel.* Yeah, I think we know each other well enough I can call ya *Rachel.*"

She backed away from him toward the sink as far as she could. "You'll never know me well enough to call me by my first name. I'm Mrs. Egan to you."

He chuckled. "In case ya haven't realized it yet —*Rachel*—I do what I want and no one stops me." He tucked the packet into the inside of his coat but kept his gun aimed at her. "Goodbye, *Rachel.* I'll be seeing you."

"Not if I see you first. Then all you'll see is the barrel of my husband's gun."

He stepped closer. "Oh, a feisty one. I like it when they fight back." He reached out to touch her with his left hand.

"That's close enough, Granger." Joshua stepped into the kitchen, his weapon trained on Billy. "Touch my wife and I'll kill you now."

Rachel turned toward Joshua but she saw that Granger didn't take his gaze off of her. "You didn't follow the rules, now you'll have to pay."

A scream sounded from the side of the house where the bedrooms were.

The sound of small feet running filled the air.

"Papa! Rachel!" Tommy yelled from behind his father.

"Stay where you are, son." Joshua issued the order without taking his gaze from Billy.

The outlaw cocked an eyebrow. "You better listen to what yer son has to say."

Joshua's eyes narrowed. "What is it, Tommy? How did you get out of Gertie's room? I'd locked you all inside."

The boy cried.

Jeffrey cried behind him.

"A man took Maggie." Tommy ran up and grabbed on to one of his father's legs.

Jeffrey grabbed the other.

Rachel's stomach turned over as if being stirred.

Her hands formed fists at her sides. “Where’s my daughter?”

Billy waved his gun, ever so slightly, back and forth in front of Rachel. “You’ll get her back as soon as I’m safely away. If you come after me, I’ll kill her and you know I’m capable.”

Rachel stared at Joshua. Their worst fear as parents realized, she thought she’d be sick.

Joshua holstered his Colt. His mouth formed a thin line and his eyes were cold as ice. “If anything happens to her, anything at all, you’ll never be rid of me. I’ll track you to the ends of the earth.”

Billy’s grin faded and he sneered, “As long as you follow the rules this time, she’s safe.” He turned to Rachel, and his grin returned. “Sorry, Rachel, but I need the head start.” He pointed his weapon directly at her heart then moved it slightly to the left and fired.

A burning like she’d never felt before emanated from her left side. As she dropped to her knees, she pressed a hand to the burn. Blood coated her palm and she looked up to her husband. “Joshua?” She fell to her side and everything turned black.

CHAPTER NINE

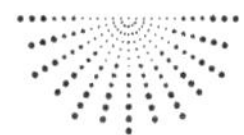

"Rachel!" Blood pumped in his ears and his heart raced as he grabbed a towel from the drawer and pressed it to her side. Then he tore cloth from her petticoat and wrapped it around her waist to keep the towel on. Next, he picked her up from where she lay on the floor and carried her to the bedroom.

How did the outlaw get in? Was it through the same window I did? I should have made sure the window was closed and locked. Why didn't I anticipate Billy would do this? His stomach churned as he realized this was probably his fault.

The boys followed him.

"Papa, Rachel bleeding," said Tommy.

"She hurt," said Jeffrey.

"Yes, she's hurt."

Joshua saw Gertie crying in her crib as he passed

her room, but he couldn't comfort his baby girl right now.

He laid Rachel on the bed and turned toward his sons. "Tommy, Jeffrey. I want you to stay in Gertie's room and I'll lock the door. Understand? I'll be right back."

Though both boys were crying, they answered with a nod.

Joshua followed them to the room and looked in. "I'll be right back, Gertie. Just be a good girl for your brothers." *Do I go to the doctor's office or the jail?* He ran out of the house to the jail since it was closest.

He burst inside.

Ezra was pinning wanted posters to the wall.

"Ezra. Go get Doc Goad and send him to my house. Rachel's been shot and I can't go myself. And after you return, gather some men. Maggie has been kidnapped."

"Say no more." Ezra grabbed his hat and was out the door running down the street toward the Carson City Hotel and Doc's office next to it.

Joshua ran home and knocked on the boy's door.

"Tommy. Jeffrey. I'm back." He unlocked the door, opened it, and found both boys sniffling.

He gathered them into his arms. "I'm so proud of you. You are such big boys and I love you very much."

"What 'bout Maggie?"

Joshua tensed. “We’ll get her back. Soon. Trust me.”

Jeffrey nodded. “We twust you, Papa. Huh, Tommy?”

“Yup, we do.”

“Good.” He gave them both a kiss on the forehead. “Now, I must see to Rachel. Can you be big boys for a while longer?”

Both boys nodded.

He glanced over to the crib where Gertie cried. She was safe. He’d come back and comfort her after making sure Rachel wasn’t bleeding too much. “Good. See if you can play with Gertie. Maybe she’ll stop crying.”

Joshua hurried to Rachel in the room next door.

“Rachel. Honey, can you hear me?” He got a towel from the commode, pulled down the cotton strip, and replaced the towel he’d pressed there. He applied pressure and hoped the bullet had gone through the muscles. He couldn’t stand the thought of her pain while Doc dug around for the lead.

Rachel moaned and grabbed for her wound.

Joshua eased away her hand.

“Joshua. He…he shot me.”

“I know and I’m so sorry. I never should have put you in the middle like I did.”

She looked away.. “Nothing to be sorry for. My fault. I should have told you first thing.” She closed her eyes. “God, I hurt.”

"I know, sweetheart. Doc Goad will be here soon."

Tommy came into the room. "Papa, someone at door. Rachel still hurt?"

"Yes, son, Rachel's still hurt." Joshua turned toward the door. "Go on back to your room. I'll answer the door and thank you for telling me."

The boy hung his head.

"Tommy? What's the matter?" asked Joshua.

"She gonna go away like my other mama?"

Rachel put a hand on Joshua's arm. "Pull the cover over me and have Tommy come here."

He covered her so Tommy couldn't see the blood.

Rachel kept her left hand on the wound and beckoned to his son with her other.

"Tommy, sweet boy, I'll be just fine. I'm not going anywhere. Okay?"

He nodded but he sniffled, too.

She wrapped her right arm around him and hugged. "Honest. I'm fine. Now, you go play with Jeffrey until your papa comes for you. Okay? Can you do that for me?"

"Uh huh and we'll play with Gertie, too."

"That's my big boy. You go on now."

As soon as the boy ran out of the room, she grimaced and pressed her head back into the pillow.

Joshua kissed her on the forehead. "I'll be right back. I'm sure that's Doc Goad."

He hurried to the front door and opened it wide.

Upon seeing the doctor, his body eased. He felt the weight on his shoulders lessen.

"Joshua, Ezra said Rachel was shot. Take me to her."

He gazed at the older man, whose silver hair belied his vigor. He may wear spectacles but nothing about him said he was an old man. His vitality put most men to shame. "Thanks for coming, Doc. Follow me."

He led the way to the bedroom.

"Well, young lady, I understand you were on the wrong end of a pistol. Let's see what we have."

Doc cut through the strips holding the towel in place and gently removed it from the wound. "Looks like the bleeding has stopped. That's a good thing. I'll need to cut your dress, though I guess it's ruined anyway. Thought I should warn you."

Rachel nodded. "Whatever you need to do is fine."

The doctor cut the dress up to the armpit and down to the hip.

"Joshua, help me turn her so I can see her back."

"Sure." He walked to the side of the bed and took her by the shoulders and turned her onto her right side. Seeing the blood and knowing it came from Rachel was almost too much to bear.

She moaned.

Joshua saw the tears run down her cheek, but she

didn't scream even though he knew the pain had to be intense.

Doc straightened. "It appears the bullet went through. I see an exit wound. Did you find a bullet where this happened?"

Joshua's hands fisted as he attempted to keep his temper under control. "I didn't look. I have a wounded wife and a kidnapped daughter, looking for a spent round is not a priority."

Doc sighed. "Of course not. What was I thinking? I'll need to clean this and then stitch both sides." He turned to Rachel. "You can't put any stress on the wound for at least two weeks. Then you'll be able to start building your strength on that side again."

"Fine. I'll make do with the right side. I still have children to take care of."

"Well, you should probably have help. Hire a girl to come in and assist you." He started digging in his bag.

I want to be here for my family. "I'll do it."

Rachel took a breath and shook her head. "You need to find Maggie as soon as possible."

Doc's eyebrows went up behind his spectacles. "Maggie? What about Maggie?"

Joshua turned toward Doc. "She was kidnapped by the same gang that shot Rachel."

Joshua walked to her and placed a kiss on her forehead. "I know. I've got Ezra rounding up a posse now. We'll find her. I'll hire a girl to come in until we get Maggie back and you heal completely."

Doc straightened and looked at Joshua. "You could talk to Merle Coleman. He's got a couple of daughters that are the appropriate age and would be happy for the money. They're good girls."

"I know Merle. He's a good man. I'll talk to him after Rachel is tended."

Doc opened his bag and brought out a brown, cup-sized bottle. "I'll give her a little chloroform when I'm ready to stitch the wound."

"I'm right here, Doc," groaned Rachel.

Doc looked down at her. "But, my dear, you are not in any condition to be making decisions for yourself."

"If it will keep me from screaming and scaring the boys, then do it."

Joshua smiled. Even in severe pain, she was thinking about his children first. He'd gotten lucky in the bride pool, as far as her caring for his kids. But he didn't forget that, if not for her, Maggie wouldn't be missing now…or would she? Would Granger have arranged her kidnapping anyway? Of course, he'd planned it all along. *We didn't hear Maggie until she was in the street. Granger walked to the back door and his gang checked the windows.* Then Joshua realized he hadn't shut the window when he came in. Maggie's kidnapping was his fault…not Rachel's. *God, what have I done?* His stomach turned as nausea threatened to overtake him. He tamped it down. Now was not the time for guilt to overcome him. Rachel needed him and so did Maggie.

Doc cleaned the wound with lye soap and water.

Tears ran in streams down Rachel's face, but she didn't make a sound.

Joshua was thankful for that. She was so strong.

The doctor took the bottle and dripped a couple of drops into a cloth. "I'm putting this cloth over your nose and mouth. I want you to breathe normally. You'll go to sleep and when you wake in a few minutes, I'll be done with your stitches, and you won't have felt a thing. You ready now?"

She closed her eyes and nodded before opening them again. "I'm ready when you are."

Doc placed the cloth on her and almost immediately her eyes closed. Then he stitched the front of the wound closed. "Joshua, turn her over, please, and hold her for me."

Joshua turned her and clenched his teeth, upon seeing the damage the bullet made coming out.

The doctor closed the exit wound with more stitches than the front.

"All right, I'll wrap her now. You'll need to check the wound every day. You can apply witch hazel, if needed. Some seepage is normal, and you should change the bandage if you see any. If a lot of blood or a yellowish discharge is present, bring her to me. I might have to open the wound and clean it again to eliminate infection."

"Will do, Doc."

Rachel began blinking her eyes and moaning. "Is it done?"

Doc smiled. "Yes, you're all done. I've given Joshua the instructions. Think hard about hiring one of the Coleman girls. You'll need her help to care for the kids especially the baby…Gertie, isn't it? I'll give you some laudanum to ease the pain. You can take half a teaspoon in half a glass of water every four hours if you need it."

Rachel nodded and turned toward Joshua. "Hire a girl and then you can concentrate on getting Maggie back."

Joshua smoothed her hair back from her forehead glad he'd been there to see her through her injury. "Whatever you want."

"I do. Now, go get Maggie."

He leaned down and kissed her. "I will." Joshua turned to Doc. "Can I leave her for a while?"

Doc prepared the laudanum and took the glass to Rachel. "Here you go. Drink this down." He helped her lean up and held the glass to her lips.

She drank the entire glass and then lay back on the pillow. She looked exhausted.

Doc packed his bag. "Sure you can leave her. She'll be out for about three to four hours. I'll talk to Merle and get one of his girls over here right away."

Joshua extended his hand.

Doc shook it.

"Thanks for coming so quickly."

"I'd appreciate it if I didn't have to come back, except maybe for dinner."

Joshua grinned. "That can be arranged after Rachel heals. How much do I owe you?"

"Five dollars ought to cover it."

Reaching into his pocket, Joshua pulled out a few bills. He plucked a five-dollar note and handed it to the doctor. "Here you are. Thanks again." He looked over at Rachel.

She had her eyes closed and looked peaceful. The laudanum appeared to be working.

The tension in Joshua's body eased.

Doc picked up his bag. "I'll go see Merle now. Expect one of the girls in about half an hour, if things work out the way I expect them to."

"I'll do that. Let me show you out." *I need to get on the trail to find Maggie before it gets cold.*

Doc Goad chuckled. "I think I can find my way. If nothing unusual happens I'll see you in ten days to remove the stitches, but I want her to continue not using that side much. Regardless of what she wants or thinks she can do, don't let her."

Joshua looked from Doc to Rachel. "Don't worry. I'll take care of her."

The doctor left.

Joshua pulled a chair to the side of the bed. He

would stay with her until the Coleman girl arrived. He hoped she hurried so he could go after Maggie and yet he wanted to stay by Rachel's side, too. Joshua knew he couldn't do both and he would go after Maggie. Rachel of all people would understand.

"Papa?"

Two little boys stood in the open doorway.

"Yes, boys." He held out a hand to them. "Come here."

They ran to him.

He pulled them onto his lap, glad for the reassurance of their warm little bodies.

Tommy sat looking down at his lap.

Jeffrey had his thumb in his mouth.

"Rachel okay? Doctor left," said Tommy, playing with a loose string on his pants.

Joshua kissed both of his sons on the top of their heads. "I don't want you boys to worry about Rachel. She will be just fine. Doc Goad fixed her right up. She'll need to rest for a couple of weeks but when she's feeling better, I can't think of anyone she'd rather see than you two." This little fib will calm them. Rachel will want to see all the children because she loves them all.

Tommy looked up at his father. "Really?"

His father smiled. "Yes, really. But for now, we have to let her sleep. So, why don't you two go back and play with Gertie?"

Jeffrey pulled his thumb from his mouth. “She’s sleepin’, too.”

“Well, go play in the living room then, but quietly. We don’t want to wake either of our sleeping girls.”

The boys slid off his lap and ran to the living room.

Their footsteps sounded like a herd of buffalo.

So much for being quiet. He turned his gaze back to Rachel. *You have to get well. I can’t lose you now.*

CHAPTER TEN

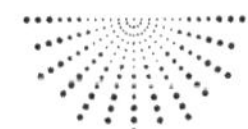

A knock sounded on the front door.

Joshua stood, picked up Rachel's hand and kissed the top. "Be right back." He walked past Gertie's room and glanced in to see if she was still asleep. Thankfully, she was.

Just before he entered the living room, he heard a bright, "Hi" from Tommy.

"Well, hi," said a young woman's voice.

He walked into the room and both of his boys stood with the door wide open, staring at a girl about sixteen.

"Hi, I'm Joshua Egan. Please come inside. Ruth, isn't it?" He stood back and held the door for her.

She stepped into the room. "Yes, sir. Ruth Coleman. Doc said you might need some help with your wife."

"Yes, let's sit in the living room." He sat on the sofa, followed by the boys.

She sat in the chair still across from the sofa, since the boys liked to build forts in the room. "These are my sons, Tommy and Jeffrey."

"I'n Tommy," he pointed at his twin. "He Jeffy."

Ruth leaned forward in the chair, resting her forearms on her thighs. "I'll do my best to remember which of you is which. I'm Ruth. Can you remember that?"

"Yup, Wuf." Tommy smiled.

"Uh huh, Wuf," echoed Jeffrey.

"Yes, that's right."

Joshua gazed at the girl. "Rachel's been injured and needs to stay abed for the next ten days. I need someone to do the cooking, cleaning, and look after my sons." He placed a hand on top of each boy's head. "And my baby daughter. The pay would be one dollar a day plus meals, if that sounds fair."

Ruth smiled wide. "Oh, yes, sir, that's more than fair."

"I'll need you to come before breakfast and stay until after dinner. Is that a problem?"

She sat in the chair, back straight, her hands clasped in her lap. "No, sir. Only to be expected."

Joshua ran a hand behind his neck. He hated having to keep the girl from home for so many hours. When Maggie returned, that would change, but he thought he'd see if Ruth wanted a permanent position.

"You might have to stay longer than the ten days. Would that be all right?"

"Yes, sir, no problem at all."

Joshua leaned back and crossed an ankle over his knee. "Good. Now, tell me a little about yourself."

She sat back and seemed to relax a bit. "I'm sixteen, and the second oldest daughter in my family. My folks are Merle and Vee Coleman and I have seven siblings. I graduated from school last May and am supposed to get married next June to Bobby Jenkins. After I turn seventeen. Maggie knows me she can probably tell you all you want to know when she gets back. I saw her with some strange men, I'm assuming they are friends of yours."

A cry rang out from down the hall.

"Ah, that would be Gertie. She's had a tough time this afternoon, but I need for you to tell me where you saw Maggie. She was kidnapped by the man who shot my wife, Rachel." Joshua stood, keeping his hands fisted. "Tell me where did you see them?"

"They rode by our house this morning headed toward Box Canyon. I know that outlaws sometimes use it for a hideout."

"Follow me. Please." Joshua turned and walked to Gertie's room. "Well, hi there, lil' darlin'. How's my Gertie girl?" *I know I need to soothe Gertie, but more importantly I need to go after Maggie.*

At eight, almost nine months, she was pulling herself up on everything, including the sides of her crib. That's where he found her. Standing, crying and holding on to the top rail of the side of her crib. She went to hold up her arms and fell to the mattress. Mad as a wet hornet, she began to bawl.

"Oh, sweetheart, you're fine. You didn't hurt anything." Joshua picked her up and found her soaked.

"Can I help you with her, sir…er…Joshua?" asked Ruth. "Yes, please. I have to go join the posse to find my daughter. You can find things in the kitchen on your own. Rachel is very organized."

"Yes, sir…er…Joshua. Can I call you Mr. Egan or Marshal Egan?"

He nodded. "Yes, that's perfectly all right, whichever you prefer."

"Marshal Egan it is. That's how I know you."

"Fine. Here, you can take Gertie. She may cry but that's fine. She'll stop as soon as you cuddle her."

"Okay."

"Oh, and Gertie's bottles are in the cupboard between the cups and the icebox. She'll need one now, so I'll let you make it. The milk should be warmed but not too hot. I have to go now and I might be gone all night. Can you stay?"

"Certainly," she whispered.

"Ruth, if you were older, I'd kiss you. Thank you for the information. You've just made my job much easier and will bring Maggie home all the sooner."

Her eyes widened. "Glad I could help. Um, will you still need me when Maggie comes home?"

"Oh, yes, don't you worry about that. We'll discuss it when I get back."

"Yes, Marshal."

Joshua headed for the door. "Lock the doors and don't let anyone but me or Doc Goad in. Okay?"

She nodded. "I understand. Do you think that bad man will be back?"

He shook his head. "I don't believe so, but I don't want to take any chances. Close all the windows, too. Never mind, I'll check them now and make sure they are locked."

When he came back, he donned his hat.

Joshua let out a deep breath. "Thank you, Ruth. You're helping me out in more ways than one."

He left out the back door and raced for the jail and his horse.

Box Canyon, Outside Carson City, Nevada Territory

Maggie knew Box Canyon was surrounded on three sides with sheer rock cliffs hundreds of feet high. With only one way in or out, they could be trapped and so could she. A small creek ran down one side of the canyon. Pine trees and scrub oak dotted the canyon floor. The scrub oak was especially tough to go by and nearly impossible to walk through as it would cling and grab your clothes.

"So, girl, do you know how to cook?"

Maggie's eyes were wide, but she knew she couldn't let fear take over. She sat on the ground, back against a fallen pine tree. Her papa would be coming for her and she had to remember that. "My name is Maggie and yes, I know how to cook."

The man with the beady eyes and missing teeth chuckled. "Well, *Maggie.* Take that rabbit," he jutted his chin toward the dead animal. "And fry it up for dinner. It's already cleaned and dressed, all you gots to do is cook it."

She looked over where the rabbit lay in the dirt. "You need to release me and I'll need water to wash off the dirt unless you want to eat fried dirt."

Billy looked at the rabbit and then toward one of the four other men around the fire. The man with the bushy red beard and crooked nose. "Dang you, Red. Ya couldn't find somethin' to lay that carcass on? Did ya hafta toss it in the dirt?"

Red ducked his head. "Sorry, Billy, I wasn't thinkin'."

"You sure as heck weren't. That happens again, you'll be eatin' yer next meal in Hell."

"Sure, sorry, Billy. It won't happen agin."

"Give her yer canteen so she can clean up that mess."

The man handed her his canteen.

"I won't rinse this until the skillet is ready." She looked around her and the camp. "There's no place to put it."

Billy sat on his haunches next to the campfire and waved a hand at her. "Whatever. Just do it."

"I'll need your skillet, lard, and salt, if you have it."

He stared at the man crouched by the fire. "Luke, get her the stuff she needs." Billy looked back at Maggie and grinned. "Even the salt."

The man with coal-black hair and a long, scraggly beard brought her the things she needed.

"Thank you."

Billy stood. "You got no need ta thank him. I'm the one who told him to give it to ya. Ya oughta be thanking me."

She shivered and tried not to let him see her shake. "I'm being polite like my mama taught me."

Billy smiled.

It was scary. Brown and missing teeth, beady eyes. He looked like the devil to Maggie. *I don't like his smile.*

"Yer mama? I remember her. She was a right nice lady."

Her heart started pounding. "You knew my mama? How?"

"Let's just say mine was the last face she saw."

Maggie furrowed her brows and tilted her head. "What do you mean? She was murdered in a stagecoach robbery? How could you—" The truth hit her right between the eyes. A knot dropped in her stomach. "You killed her, didn't you?"

His grin widened. "I can't tell a lie. I had to kill her, she just wouldn't shut up. Are ya like yer mother? I hope not. I really don't want to kill ya, but I will." His smile faded to a frown. "If ya don't shut up and just cook dinner."

"Fine. Are you going to cut it up, or do you trust me enough with a knife to let me do it?"

Billy handed her the big knife at his waist. "I don't trust you at all but I figure you can't outrun a bullet…if'n ya try somethin'." He patted the pistol at his side.

Maggie followed his hand movement with her gaze and swallowed hard. She had to escape. She had to get back home, make this nightmare end and the sooner, the better.

She cut up the rabbit into pieces and fried it, making sure not to burn it. Maggie didn't want to give Billy a reason to shoot her.

When the food was done, she removed the skillet from the fire. "Here's your meat."

Billy stood and walked over to her…reached down…and picked up his knife, wiped the blade on his pants, and replaced it in the scabbard.

"Looks good." He picked up a back leg with his fingers and set it in one of the tin plates setting by the fire.

None of the other men moved.

He took a bite and carried his plate back to the other side of the campfire. "You all can eat now." Billy returned to his haunches.

The men all crowded each other trying to get to the frying pan and the other back leg. It had the most meat on it. Once each man had a piece, they went back to their spots around the fire. One piece was left in the skillet.

Billy picked up the last bit of rabbit. "You done real good lil' girl. I probably should have let you have a piece but it was just too good fer me not to eat it."

Maggie jutted her chin out. "I wasn't hungry anyway."

He laughed and was joined by the other four men in the group.

She sat against a fallen tree and crossed her arms over her chest for warmth as the sun went down. Keeping her eyes on Billy, she hoped he would fall asleep and the other men would follow. Maggie would even pretend to go to sleep, if necessary.

Her escape hinged on them leaving her legs untied, and so far, that was what they were doing. When she escaped, she'd go to the Coleman ranch, they'd passed it on the way here. If she could just get away tonight.

CHAPTER ELEVEN

Joshua led his posse of five of the best marksmen in town, including Merle Coleman.

It was barely dawn, and the sky was still black with a sliver of orange rising. The canyon entrance faced east. With the sun at their back and this early in the morning, they would still be hard to see.

Merle had come into town after his eldest daughter said she saw Maggie riding into Box Canyon with five men. Merle knew that couldn't be right, but he couldn't do anything alone, so he rode to the marshal's office.

The group hit the entrance to the canyon and dismounted. They would walk the rest of the way. Horses made too much noise and Joshua didn't want Billy or any of his gang to be alerted to the posse's presence. He scanned the rocks near the entrance but didn't see anyone.

Walking slow, as quiet as five men could be, Joshua and his men entered the canyon. About halfway into the canyon he saw Billy's camp. They had Maggie bound and gagged. Joshua's relief nearly dropped him to his knees and he hoped she was okay and Billy hadn't hurt her.

The man was scum and Joshua knew he would kill Maggie in a heartbeat if he thought he could get out unscathed. Or he'd keep her as a hostage and be able to ride out, even if it was just him. He had no loyalty to any of the men he rode with. He'd probably replaced the man he killed at the same time as Frank Cowell. Joshua swore he would not get away this time.

His men spread out ringing in the outlaws.

"Billy Granger," shouted Joshua, aiming his rifle at Billy's head. "You're surrounded. I've brought the best sharpshooters and each one has one of your men in his sights. I have you in mine. You so much as make a move for your gun or toward Maggie, and you're dead. You made a mistake shooting my wife and kidnapping my daughter. Give up now, Billy, or die. The choice is yours but you better decide fast. You've got until I reach ten. One…two…three…"

Billy sat up and looked around, then he put up his hands and so did his men.

Joshua and the rest of the posse moved in and captured the gang.

Merle Coleman untied Maggie while Joshua kept his rifle trained on Billy.

Billy stayed where he was and glared at Maggie. "I knew you'd be trouble."

Maggie smiled and stood. "You never should have messed with my papa."

"Come to me, Maggie, sweet."

She ran to him and hugged him around the waist. "I knew you'd come. I just knew you'd find me."

"I'll always find you. Ruth Coleman is the one who alerted me and then her father showed up at the jail."

Joshua kept his weapon trained on Billy. "Merle, take Billy's gun."

"And the big knife, too," said Maggie pointing at the outlaw's waist.

Coleman took both weapons and shoved Billy in front of him, toward one of the other men who tied the wrists of each gang member. They would leave their legs free so they could walk to the end of the canyon and then ride.

Joshua and his men would ride the gang's horses until they reached their own. He finally lowered his rifle and hugged Maggie.

"Everyone will be happy to have you back."

She pulled back and looked up at him. "Except

Rachel. She probably won't be happy. I haven't been very nice to her."

Joshua squeezed her shoulder. "I'm sure she'll be very happy to have you back and when she gets better, you can start over."

Maggie frowned. "Gets better? What's the matter with her?"

He glanced at the rest of the posse and then back at his daughter. "Billy shot her in order to make his getaway. She's bedridden for at least two weeks and will need your help even after that. She'll be weak and sore and unable to do a lot of her chores. I've hired Ruth Coleman to help, and she'll stay as long as we need her to."

Maggie's eyes filled with tears. "Was she shot because of me?"

Joshua knelt so he could see her face. "You had nothing to do with it. Hear me? Nothing."

"But—"

"No buts. Nothing you did or didn't do caused him to shoot her. He did it because he's a vicious, cold-blooded killer. Nothing more. Okay?" He winced, hating that he was using such blunt language with her, but he didn't want Maggie to have any thoughts that she had anything to do with Rachel being shot.

She nodded. "Okay. I'll help her as much as I can." Tears made rivers down her face. "I'm sorry

I've been so mean. She's a really nice lady, you know."

He smiled. "I know. I like her, too."

"Do you love her?"

His daughter's question took him aback. Did he love her? He'd asked himself this question before and still didn't have a good answer. Sometimes he thought he did and then he'd remember Marjorie. He felt like he was being unfaithful to her, to her memory.

"I don't know."

"You know, Mama would have been okay with you finding love again. She was that kind of person."

"That's very observant for someone your age."

She put her head down but he thought he saw a smile. Then she looked back up. "I heard Mrs. Peabody telling Mama that her husband wouldn't want her to live alone. Mama said she wouldn't want you to either and knew you felt the same way about her."

Joshua hugged his daughter. He felt like Marjorie was taking care of him from beyond.

"Mama taught me a lot of things. Kindness is one of them. One I forgot to follow with Rachel. Do you think she'll forgive me?"

Hearing Maggie's words of remorse, he was reminded of Marjorie. They could have come from his deceased wife's mouth. "I'm sure she will. She understands how hard it is for you to accept her. You were very close to your mother."

She hugged him again. “I miss her.”

He wrapped his arms around her. “I know. We all do. But just because we miss and love your mother doesn’t mean we can’t love Rachel. You just taught me that.”

Maggie gazed at him, eyes wide. “I did?”

He smiled and kissed her forehead. “You did.” He stood. “Let’s get you home.”

“I’m ready.”

He’d just assured his daughter that Rachel would forgive her. Now, he wondered if she would forgive him.

Rachel awoke slowly. Her side hurt something awful. She felt where it hurt and found a bandage. Then she remembered. Billy Granger shot her. He needed the time for his getaway and shot her knowing Joshua would have to take care of her.

He’d had to take time from his search for Maggie, because of her. Would he forgive her for that? She closed her eyes. When she opened them again, she looked around. The light coming through the window, cast long shadows on the wall. It was late. Where were the kids? Joshua? What if Maggie was hurt?

Rachel couldn’t bear to contemplate anything else.

She heard a baby's giggle and turned toward it.

"Hi. Glad to see you're awake," said a pretty, brown-haired girl.

The help Joshua had hired.

"Who are you?"

"Ruth Coleman. I'm here to help you and when my mama was under the effect of laudanum she sometimes didn't want to wake up, I'd bring in one of the babies and as soon as she heard the giggle or cooing or whatever sound the baby made, she would wake. I thought I'd try it with you, and it worked."

Rachel smiled. It had worked. She'd heard her baby, heard Gertie giggling. Nothing was as beautiful as a baby's giggle.

"Ruth. You did say it was Ruth, right?"

"Yes, ma'am."

"Where's Joshua? The kids?"

"First the boys are fine. They've eaten dinner and are in their nightshirts and ready for bed. I'm sure they'd like to see you, if you're up to it."

"Not tonight, I don't feel well enough. As a matter-of-fact I think I need more laudanum, but I don't want to take as much. I don't think I'm thinking straight right now. What's your name again?"

"Ruth. It's okay. Mama was the same way. I'm allowed to give you half a teaspoon in water every four hours, but there's no reason we can't cut that down so it just helps with the pain and doesn't make you sleep. We did that with Mama. Maybe do it by the drop. Start with five drops and see if that works. If not, we'll try seven, and so forth. Want to try it?"

"Yes, please."

"Good. Let me put Gertie in her crib, and I'll get it for you."

"You can leave her with me."

Wrinkles formed on Ruth's forehead as she frowned and shook her head. She shifted Gertie to her other hip. "No, I can't. What if something happened? You don't have the strength to deal with her."

Rachel let out a deep breath and nodded. "You're right. If she cries a little, she cries a little."

"Yes, exactly. I'll get her again after you get your medicine."

Ruth left.

Rachel heard Gertie cry. She sounded so forlorn. Poor baby. *She needs me now more than ever. And I can't do anything for her.*

The girl returned with a half glass of water. "Sorry about the taste. Mama said it is awful, and she couldn't wait to stop taking it." She handed the glass to Rachel.

She took it with her right hand and downed the water without stopping. "Now, I need a fresh glass of water without the laudanum."

"Certainly." Ruth walked to the bureau and filled the glass from the pitcher. "Here you go. You must be very thirsty."

Rachel nodded. "I feel totally dried out."

Gertie stopped crying.

That's odd. Maybe the boys are entertaining her.

Joshua entered the room, carrying Gertie, with Maggie right behind him.

Rachel would rejoice if she could. "Oh, good, you found her. Are you all right, Maggie?"

"I'm fine, but you—" Her eyes filled with tears. "I'm so sorry. I won't be mean to you anymore."

Rachel beckoned her to the bed. "Come here."

The girl rushed to the bedside.

Pulling her in for a hug, Rachel felt the child's tears on her chest. "Shh. It's all right. You have the right to honor your mother. I know you miss her, and I don't want to replace her, but I'd be thrilled if you and I could be friends. Will that work for you?"

Maggie raised her head. "You really want to be my friend?"

Smiling, Rachel tucked a lock of hair behind Maggie's ear. "Yes. I really do."

"I'd like that, too."

"Good, now we've totally ignored your father and Ruth." She turned toward Joshua. "I'm so glad you found her quickly. Ruth has been taking very good care of the children and me. What time is it? Shouldn't you be having breakfast or lunch? I don't know what time it is, mostly that it's daylight and I see more sun in the eastern window than the west."

"I have eggs, sausage, and biscuits in the warming

oven," Ruth piped up. "I'd hoped you would return this morning."

Joshua turned to Ruth. "You've done a great job. I look forward to your work in the coming days."

The girl blushed under his praise. "Thank you, Marshal Egan."

"You and Maggie will have this house running smoothly while Rachel recovers." He fixed his gaze on Rachel. "Do you hear that? You don't have to worry about anything. The girls will have it under control."

"I hear it, and right now, I'm very happy to let them do everything."

Ruth went to Rachel. "Do you want the other half teaspoon of laudanum?"

Joshua walked over and sat in the rocker next to the bed and narrowed his eyes. "You cut your dose in half?"

Rachel tried to turn over and grimaced. "Yes, the full dose makes me go to sleep, but it helps the pain more. I'll take the full dose from now on. I don't like this pain."

He stood, bent and kissed her forehead. "That's my girl."

Her heart fluttered and her eyes widened. "Your girl?"

Joshua smiled. "Yes, my girl." He turned and left the room with Gertie.

Ruth returned to her bedside with a glass of water.

"Here's your medicine. I'll get you a fresh glass of water when you finish this."

Rachel was still flabbergasted by Joshua's words.

Maggie gave Rachel a gentle hug. "I'll go check on the boys."

"I'm glad you're home. Billy Granger is a vicious man, and I worried for you."

The child looked at her feet and clasped her hands in front of her. "I thought you'd be happy I was gone."

"Oh, no, sweetheart." Rachel reached out and took Maggie's hand. "You can be as angry and mean as you want with me, and I will always love and want you."

"Thank you for not giving up on me."

Rachel squeezed Maggie's hand. "Never. Now, you go on and take care of your brothers and sister. And remember I love you…no matter what."

The girl nodded, turned, and left the room.

It was just as well, the laudanum was taking effect and she was suddenly so sleepy.

"Don't fight it, Mrs. Egan," said Ruth. "Let the medicine work and you'll heal faster. Mama tried to do what you are and sometimes it worked, but she was in a lot of pain then, too. She said she just worked her way through it. This was after she had my little brother. The birth was hard on her."

"I've heard they can be sometimes." Rachel's

eyes kept closing and she struggled to keep them open while she talked to Ruth.

"I should go help Maggie. I think it's laundry day."

"It is. I don't envy you. I hate laundry day."

"I'll check back later, I think you should rest."

Rachel nodded. "You're right."

After Ruth left, Rachel turned to her back, and the pain nearly made her call out, but she refused to let it. Her yell would scare the kids.

She couldn't let go of Joshua's words. "My girl." What in the world did he mean?

CHAPTER TWELVE

Ten days had passed and Rachel could get her stitches out. She dressed in a blouse and skirt instead of a dress. She wanted to make it easy for the doctor to remove the stitches.

Joshua lay on the bed, dressed except for his boots, and watched her. "I want the doctor to check you out today. I want to know why your menses have stopped."

"I'm telling you, it's just nerves."

He sat on the side of the bed and pulled on his boots. "That may be but I want to know for sure."

"Oh, all right." She struggled with the buttons at her waist. "All that lying in bed has made me gain weight. I can barely button my skirt, and even my blouse seems tight." She tugged at the front buttons that gaped.

Joshua chuckled.

"What's so funny? If I get much fatter, I'll need all new clothes."

"Then we'll buy you new clothes. I like a little extra meat on you. You're definitely filling out. I can tell in your bosom."

Rachel's face heated, and her cheeks burned. "You shouldn't say such things."

He walked to her, turned her to face him and then wrapped his arms around her waist, pulling her close. "Does it embarrass you that I enjoy our private time together?"

"No, but it's not polite to talk about intimate things."

He laughed and then waggled his brows before lowering his head to kiss her. "The last thing I want to do during our special time together is be polite."

She shook her head. "You're a crazy man."

"Crazy about my wife."

Eyes wide, she jerked up her head and looked at him. "Crazy about me?"

He frowned. "Yes, I'm crazy about you. I want us both to be happy in our marriage. I want you to forgive me for my obtuseness and my accusations."

"There is nothing for me to forgive. You're the one who needs to forgive me. I brought Billy Granger down on our house and our family. He kidnapped Maggie because of me. He even shot me because of what I'd done."

Tears filled her eyes. *Gosh darn it. Why am I*

crying all the time? It seems like the least little thing can set me off. This has got to stop.

Rachel stepped out of the house and immediately shivered in the cold air. Walking to the doctor's office warmed her a little.

Doctor Goad's nurse started to usher her into a room.

"I'd like Joshua to come with me, please."

The nurse raised her brows but nodded. "Will you both follow me back to the surgery, and then Doc'll take out those stitches."

The doctor came in almost as soon as the nurse left.

He walked to the counter where a pitcher and basin were sitting and washed his hands. "I knew you'd be in today. I was sure you'd want those stitches out as soon as possible. Get up on the table, please." He looked over at Joshua. "Are you staying?"

Joshua nodded. "I am. She wants me here."

"That is most unusual but as you wish, you may stay. Sit in the chair against the wall and don't interfere."

"I won't get in your way." Joshua sat in the chair and crossed his arms over his chest.

She hopped up on the examination table and swung her legs. "Doctor, my husband wants you to check me and see why my menses have stopped."

Doc cocked his head and grinned. “Usually, it’s because you’re expecting.”

“That’s impossible. You see, I’m barren. I was married to my late husband for nine years and never got pregnant.”

The doctor shrugged. “That isn’t necessarily you. Your husband could have been unable to sire children.”

She shook her head. “Oh, no, he was sure it was me.”

“I’ll check you out after I remove the sutures. Please remove your blouse and undergarment.”

Rachel unbuttoned the blouse and shrugged it off, followed by her chemise. She’d given up wearing a corset after the first week of trying to do her chores in one.

She bent her right arm and rested it on top of her head.

Doc quickly snipped all the thread that held her skin together while it healed.

Rachel was surprised it didn’t hurt. “That was fast.”

“They’re easy to take out, it’s the putting in that hurts. Now, I want you to remove your bloomers and lie back on the table.”

She complied. Having been to so many doctors when she was married to Claude, she knew the procedure the doctor would do to check her. Claude had been so sure it was her, he’d taken her to about twenty different doctors over the course of the first two years they were married. The answer was always the same. Physically she was fine but since she didn't get pregnant, she must be barren. She'd cried for days after each checkup for the first year. After that she was resigned to the fact…she would never have children.

"First I want to see if your body has changed."

He pressed on her stomach, through her clothes to check her uterus. Then he checked her privates by reaching under her skirt and checking by feel. Her modesty was always preserved.

I don't know why I'm putting up with this. I know the problem is just nerves.

Doc covered her with her skirt. "You can redress now."

"Well, Doc? What's happening to her?" asked Joshua.

Doc smiled wide. "I'd say you'll be new parents in about six months based on the time you've been married."

Rachel dropped her bloomers and hung onto the table. "I'm pregnant. Truly?"

Doc put his hands in his pockets and rocked back on his heels. "Yes, my dear, truly."

Her wobbly legs gave way.

Joshua was there to catch her.

She looked up at him.

Grinning from ear to ear, Joshua stood at the end of the table.

"Even after we discussed the possibility." She accused. "You knew what he would find."

"I was pretty sure when you were throwing up every day. Marjorie did that her first few months, too. Then, when you had trouble getting into your clothes this morning, I was sure. But I knew you wouldn't believe me, so Doc had to confirm your condition."

She touched her stomach. *Pregnant. Never in a million years would I have thought the infertile one was Claude all this time.* "We'll have two in diapers, and we need another crib. A bassinet will work for a few months, but we definitely will need the crib. Gertie is too young to go into a regular bed. Do you think Maggie will mind sharing her room with either Gertie or this new baby?"

He put his finger to her lips. "Shh. Put on your bloomers so we can go home."

"Yes, of course." She snatched her bloomers off the floor and donned them in record time. Rachel couldn't wait to tell the children they would have a new little sister or brother.

Joshua extended his hand to her. "I'm sure she'll be thrilled, and I'm sure she'll want to share with the new baby."

She took his hand.

Doc pulled out his pocket watch. "Yes, yes. It's all well and good. You two can decide these things at home and you have six months to decide. But right now I have another patient to see."

Joshua put his hand out. "Thanks, Doc. You've given us some great news today. What do I owe you?"

"Well," the doctor pulled on his chin. "Taking out the stitches was included with the price of putting them in. So, you only owe me for the exam. That'll be three dollars."

Joshua reached in his pocket and pulled out several coins. He gave the doctor three gold dollar coins.

"Cheap at twice the price," he said.

Doc laughed. "Well, in that case—"

"Just kidding, Doc. Just kidding."

Rachel finished dressing while the men talked.

Joshua turned to her. "Are you ready?"

"As much as I'll ever be," she replied, smoothing her skirt. She was really going to have a baby. June. She would have her baby around the end of May if it was on time.

Her hands shook and her legs were still wobbly, but she managed to take Joshua's hand and walk out of the doctor's office on her own two feet.

He squeezed her hand. "Are you all right?"

A horse and buggy, driven by Mrs. Peabody, the preacher's wife, drove by. "Hello, Joshua and Rachel," she called as she drove past.

Rachel waved. Then she turned to Joshua. "Yes. No." She grinned. "I still can't believe it. All this time, I thought I couldn't have children and the reason was that monster, not me."

"Are you happy?"

"I'm overjoyed." She and Joshua passed by the butcher shop and waved at Mr. Pflugner, the owner.

Rachel leaned into Joshua's side.

He let go of her hand and instead put an arm around her shoulders. "I'm glad you're happy. I know you always said you wanted a baby but were barren and I wasn't sure how you'd take the news."

She wrapped her arm around his waist. "How could I be anything but thrilled? The babe should be here the end of May. A summer baby. What about you? We already have four children, do you want a fifth?"

They stopped in front of the house.

He turned and took her by the hands, kissing the top of each one. "I want as many children as the Good Lord sees fit to give us."

"Good, because I have a feeling this one won't be our last since I know you're keeping me."

"Oh, I'm definitely keeping you." He pulled her close and kissed her deeply.

"Come on," Maggie's voice sounded from behind. "Do you two have to do that *all* the time?"

Joshua rested his forehead against Rachel's and chuckled. "We've been found out."

"I came to see if you wanted cold sandwiches for lunch. I've been watching for you to get back. Did you get your stitches out? Did Doc tell you not to do anything for a while?"

Rachel turned in Joshua's arms to face Maggie. She rested her arms on top of his at her waist. "Actually, Doc forgot to tell me what I could and couldn't do, so I'll just take it easy for a while longer, I think. He mentioned it before, maybe he didn't think he needed to say it again."

The skin between Maggie's brows wrinkled, and she nodded. "Doc knows what he's talkin' about. Besides…" She put her arms behind her back and swayed to and fro. "Ruth and I have everything under control. We have the chores split and on the big ones like laundry day, we both do it. We have to change the beds that day, anyway, and that's a lot of work."

Rachel smiled. "You're right, it is a lot of work. Are you sure you and Ruth can handle it?"

The girl nodded fast. "Oh, yes, very sure."

"Well, I guess I'll just have to follow the doctor's orders then and take it easy for another two weeks."

Maggie grinned. "You can take longer than that. I mean, if you want to."

Rachel walked over to the child. "Are you telling me that I'm not needed anymore?"

Rachel shot him daggers with her gaze.

He coughed to cover his mirth.

"Do you like having Ruth here?"

"Yes, it's nice having her here. I like having someone to talk to."

"So you don't need me, after all."

Maggie looked stricken. "Oh, no. I would never

say you aren't needed. Me and the little kids need you but—"

"But you're having fun with Ruth."

She nodded. "We are having fun and I'm learning the right way to take care of a family."

Rachel knelt to be nearer to eye level with Maggie and winced at the movement. "It's okay to have fun while you're learning and while you're working. Getting enjoyment out of what you do is wonderful."

"But most of the women I overhear talk about how they hate it and wish they didn't have to do housework."

"Those women were probably never happy to begin with. Don't put any stock in what they say. As you've found out housework isn't easy but if you and Ruth continue to be happy with your work, you'll make wonderful marriages that, I would bet, you'll be happy in, too."

Maggie threw her arms around Rachel. "Thank you."

She laughed and stopped herself from moaning in pain at the extra weight of Maggie's hug. "You're welcome. By the way, how do you feel about sharing your bedroom?"

Stepping back, Maggie looked askance at Rachel. "Sharing my room with who?"

"Well, that's the thing," said Joshua. "We don't know yet?"

"If you don't know, then why'd you ask me to share my room?"

Rachel smiled and looked down at the little girl, who wasn't so little after all. "You see, the arrival won't be until around the end of May or first of June."

Maggie furrowed her brows and then her eyes widened. "Are you having a baby? No, you couldn't be. You said you couldn't have babies. I heard you tell Papa."

Rachel shrugged. "I guess I was wrong." Then she smiled. "So, what do you think? Will you share your room with either Gertie or the new baby?"

The girl hugged Rachel and then ran to her father. "I wouldn't mind sharing at all. Can the new baby stay with me?"

Joshua clasped her in his embrace. "We were hoping you'd say that. I'll get another crib and put it in your room wherever you want it."

"Next to my bed. Then, if the baby wakes up, I can get to it fast."

Rachel shook her head. "For the first few months, we'll have the infant in our bedroom in a bassinette. Then, when the baby is ready, it'll move into your room."

Maggie's shoulders slumped.

"What's the matter?" asked Rachel.

She shrugged. "I just thought I'd be taking care of the baby all the time."

Joshua smiled and squeezed her shoulders. "Let's go into the house to talk. It's cold out here."

"Yes, let's." Rachel stood and rubbed her arms up and down over her coat.

"Okay," said Maggie. "I'm cold, too."

They went in all the way to the kitchen.

The boys were playing in their room.

Once seated at the table, Joshua resumed their conversation. "For as long as possible, Rachel will take care of feeding the baby. If, and when, the child is weaned and takes a bottle, then you can do the feedings when you're not in school. We've been lax about your lessons."

Maggie perked up. "I guess that's okay. Can I still play with the baby?"

"Sure. But you mustn't forget to play with and love on Gertie. She'll be jealous of the new baby, anyway, so we have to remember to include her in everything. And don't tell the boys, yet. We want the news to be a surprise when we tell them tomorrow morning. Okay?"

The little girl straightened her spine and jutted out her chin. "You can count on me." She stood. "Ruth will be here shortly and I promise not to tell her either."

"Thank you," said Rachel.

Maggie headed out of the kitchen leaving her father and Rachel alone.

She stood and waited for Joshua to take her hand

and maybe to continue the kissing they'd been doing before Maggie came outside.

He pulled her back into his arms.

Looked like she wouldn't be disappointed.

"Rachel." He dipped his head and took her lips with his, kissing her deeply. When he pulled back, he stared down at her with his mouth crooked up a little at one corner.

"What?" She narrowed her eyes. "What's happening with you? What don't I know?"

"I'll tell you tonight." He took her hand in his and kissed the top before heading out of the kitchen.

Great. Now I'll be on pins and needles all day long.

CHAPTER THIRTEEN

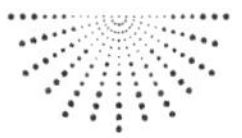

The day couldn't get over quickly enough for Rachel. She still couldn't imagine what Joshua wanted to talk about that he couldn't say when they were outside or around the kids.

She couldn't think what it could be.

After dinner, both she and Joshua put the children to bed. They each read from *The Tales of Mother Goose.* The kids loved the stories. They also read from *Robinson Crusoe* or *Gulliver's Travels.* Both of these were Rachel's favorites, but she wouldn't admit it. According to Claude, ladies weren't supposed to be interested in adventure stories. Little did he know she read them anyway when she was cooking since he would never degrade himself to enter the kitchen.

Maggie was the last to be put to bed. Once Joshua tucked her in, he kissed her forehead.

Rachel did the same for the boys and Gertie, but

she'd always kept her distance from Maggie because the child wanted nothing to do with her on such a personal level.

As she turned to go, Maggie called out.

"Rachel, would you kiss me goodnight like you do the boys and Gertie?"

Turning, she smiled. "I would like that very much." She walked back to the girl, bent down and kissed her forehead. When Maggie reached up and hugged her around the neck, she was shocked to her toes.

"Goodnight, Maggie. I'll see you in the morning."

"Goodnight, Rachel. Goodnight, Papa."

Rachel preceded Joshua to their bedroom and, for the first time since they were married, he locked the door. That in itself was unusual, but the grin he had on his face when he looked at her was not his normal grin. "What do you want, Joshua?"

"Just this." He dropped to one knee and took her left hand in his. "Rachel Egan, will you do me the great honor of becoming my wife? You already wear my ring, but I want you to know I would choose you over every other woman on Earth. I love you, with my heart and soul."

Her throat was tight and her heart raced as happy tears filled her eyes. "Oh, Joshua. I love you, too. I have for so very long but had resigned myself to never having the feeling returned. You are the only man I've ever loved."

He stood and put his arms around her waist. "I'm glad to hear it. I would have worried if you'd told me you'd been in love with Claude."

"Never." She shook her head and involuntarily shivered. "I feared Claude and simply did my best not to provoke him. But love him? It's more like I loathed him."

"I thank the Lord every day for sending you…to the kids and especially to me. I want to get married again, this time in the church with all of our family and friends there to celebrate with us. And you can wear that pretty green dress you like so much and that you wore the first time."

She nodded as her tears ran down her cheeks.

He kissed her.

Rachel thought he must love her if he could kiss her, wet face and all.

Joshua released her only to unbutton her dress, slide it off her shoulders, and let it fall to the floor in a heap.

Taking the hint, she unbuttoned his shirt and, as quickly as she could, removed the garment, adding it to the growing pile of clothes.

The mutual undressing continued until both were in their glory, and Joshua carried her to the bed.

"I want to make love to you, real love, because now I'm sure what that is. I loved Marjorie, but it was a young love, never having matured. We were sweethearts in school, and it was assumed we'd marry, but with you—I don't know. The things I feel are so much deeper and richer than anything before. I love you and I don't think I can ever tell you enough."

She laughed. "I can never hear those words enough, but Maggie will think we're being too affectionate."

He grinned. "Maggie can think what she wants. I only care what you think."

She cupped his face. "You *know* what I think." Rachel kissed him, putting all her love into it.

Soon, he took control of the kiss. When he stopped, they were both breathing hard.

"Wow, that was some kiss." She smiled.

"You think that was something, just wait until you feel what's next."

Rachel giggled.

He waggled his brows. "Careful, you'll wake the children."

The next morning, Rachel could not stop smiling for the life of her.

Maggie stopped washing the eggs. "Why are you smiling so much?"

Rachel grinned. "I'm just happy. Can't I be happy?"

Her eldest daughter furrowed her brows, though they were so light a blonde, if her forehead hadn't wrinkled, Rachel would never have known the brows changed shape.

"Yeah, I guess so."

"Good. Now, finish with the eggs, and I'll get the bacon started and the pancake batter mixed."

"Pancakes? Instead of biscuits?" She shook her head. "Now, I know something is not right."

Rachel looked behind her and then beckoned Maggie over. "Remember, we're telling the boys about the new baby this morning. I wanted breakfast to be a little special."

Maggie turned a lovely shade of pink. "I forgot about the baby."

Rachel laughed. "Well, that made it easier to not tell the boys about him. I've decided to call it *him*. I don't like the idea of our baby being an it. What do you think?"

The girl took an old child's hairbrush and scrubbed the eggs. It was the only kind of brush that was not likely to break the shell. "I think it's a good idea. I much prefer *him* to *it*, but I think we could call him a girl…er…*her* instead."

Happy with the easy conversation, Rachel smiled. "I'm open to that idea. We'll start calling it, *her*."

Joshua walked into the kitchen carrying Gertie and with two little boys, still in their nightshirts following, rubbing their eyes and yawning. "Calling who her?"

Rachel widened her eyes, jutted her chin toward the boys, and shook her head.

"Oh, right. Not yet."

"The coffee is ready. I'll get you a cup and then I'll get Gertie her bottle."

He came over and gave her a kiss. "Thanks."

"You're welcome." She kissed Gertie. "Hi there, sweetie. How are you this morning?"

Suddenly shy, Gertie laid her head on her papa's shoulder.

"Looks like someone isn't quite awake yet." Rachel glanced at the boys. "Several someones."

From the sink, Maggie called out, "Do you want me to scramble all these eggs?"

Rachel turned toward her daughter. Maggie was as sure of being her daughter as Rachel was being the girl's mother. "Leave out four. I think I'll bake a cake or some cookies, or," she chuckled. "Maybe both."

"I vote for both." Joshua and Maggie chimed in together.

"Okay. We'll see how the day progresses."

"Ruth will be in shortly. She's milking the cow," said Maggie. "We'll take care of the kids and the meals, and you can just bake. Even Doc would agree that's okay."

Joshua nodded. "I do believe you're right, daughter mine."

Maggie cocked her head and stared at her father.

Rachel covered the smile she couldn't hide with

her fingers. Maggie obviously hadn't seen this playful side of her father, at least recently.

Recovering, Rachel gave Joshua his coffee and handed Gertie's bottle to Maggie. "Will you please feed her for me?"

"Sure. Come on Gertie girl." She picked up her sister from her father and went into the living room.

Rachel leaned back against the sink. "She's so good with the baby."

Joshua placed his arms around Rachel's waist and drew her to him. "She always has been. With her siblings, she hasn't a jealous bone in her body. With you, it was different. Even then, I don't think it was so much jealousy as it was fear. She was afraid you'd replace Marjorie."

She sighed. "I know. And I did try to take that into account in my dealings with her." Rachel paused, and then she tilted her head just a little and turned her gaze after Maggie. "Isn't it strange that the man who took my beloved brother from me would also give me my most precious daughter?"

Joshua's arms tightened around her waist. "Don't give that animal any good thoughts. He's evil through and through. That's the only thing to be said for him. "

"I'm not excusing him. He is the devil personified; I just thought the coincidence was odd."

"You're right, but I will never get over what he took from us."

"Nor will I. I promise you. I want to see justice done for our family members."

The boys sat at the table, and Tommy put his head on it.

"He tired," said Jeffrey.

Rachel took the eggs Maggie had scrambled and poured them in the hot skillet. She gazed at Tommy. "It does look that way. When the food is done, Joshua can wake him up to eat and listen to what we have to say."

Rachel watched the bacon while Maggie cooked the scrambled eggs.

When everything was ready, Rachel nodded toward Tommy. "You can wake him up now."

Joshua nodded and gently shook his son's shoulder. "Tommy, wake up."

"Papa?"

"It's me. You must wake up and eat breakfast."

"Okay." He laid his head down again.

"Tommy! Wake up."

The boy sat up but started to put his head down.

Rachel thought he reacted to Joshua's sharp tone rather than the actual words.

"Today we're having pancakes with our eggs. Don't you want some, Tommy?"

He nodded vigorously and was suddenly wide awake. "Uh huh."

"Good." She poured the batter into two hot skillets. The first batch, she served to the boys and Joshua.

Ruth came in carrying a bucket of fresh milk.

Rachel pointed at the table. "Have a seat, Ruth. You too, Maggie. These pancakes are almost done and they are best when hot."

She did another batch. "Anyone else want more pancakes or eggs or bacon before I sit?"

She received a chorus of nos and one yes from Joshua, which she expected. Rachel carried the skillet to the table and served her husband more pancakes. After she sat, she took a cooled pancake and set it on Gertie's highchair tray.

The baby picked it up and happily took a bite, Rachel cleared her throat.

"Children and Ruth, your papa and I have some news."

Maggie sat back and grinned.

"We are having a baby, which will be here around the first of June next year."

Ruth jumped up, hurried to Rachel, and gave her a hug. "A baby! That's wonderful."

Joshua grinned, both of his dimples showing. "What do you boys think about that?"

"Can't we get a puppy instead?" asked Tommy. "We gots a baby."

Rachel laughed.

Joshua joined in.

So did Ruth and Maggie.

Rachel grinned. "Well? Papa, can we get a puppy, too?"

He shook his head. "I suppose we can get a puppy. But you kids have to take care of it. Feed it. Water it. Play with it. Everything. Your mother and I will not be responsible for your puppy. Understand?"

"Yay!" shouted Tommy.

"Yay!" echoed Jeffrey.

"We'll take good care of it," said Maggie. "I promise."

"Our sheepdog just had puppies," said Ruth. "They'll be old enough to give away in about six weeks. Papa doesn't like to keep them too long because we all get too attached to them."

Maggie bounced in her chair. "Can we get one of the puppies? Please, Papa, please?"

Joshua laughed. "All right. I'll talk to Merle and see what we can do."

Rachel chuckled as a chorus of cheers issued forth from the children. She was a little disappointed they weren't as enthusiastic about the baby but understood that puppies were more important to children.

"Okay." Rachel clapped her hands. "Now that we have that settled, finish your breakfast. It's a long time until lunch."

They all dug in, including Rachel. This was a mistake. Halfway through her meal, she suddenly jumped up and ran to the sink, where she lost all the food she'd just eaten.

Joshua hurried to her. "Are you all right? You should probably have only crackers in the mornings until the vomiting passes. Marjorie had this happen, too. Especially with the twins. Crackers and tea were all she could keep down for about three months. Yours should be passing soon, I think."

Rachel grabbed a dish towel, wet it from the pump, and ran the cold cloth over her face, leaving her mouth for last.

Joshua rubbed her back. "Better?"

"I think so." She nodded. "I'm not eating anything else until lunch. This only happens in the morning."

"That's the way it was with Marjorie."

Ruth came over to the sink. "Are you okay, Mrs. Egan?"

"Yes, thank you, Ruth."

"When Mama has this, and she has had it with every baby, she eats dry toasted bread in the mornings and tea, like the marshal says."

"I'll give it a try."

"I'm sure it will help. I'll make you some."

Ruth went to the cupboard, got a cup, placed tea leaves in the bottom, and ladled hot water from the bucket on the stove into it. She set it on the table at Rachel's plate before sitting to finish her own meal.

The boys watched Rachel, their lips quivering.

"I'm fine, boys. See?" She stood and walked back to the table. "Everything is fine."

"We don't like to see you sick, Mama," said Jeffrey, his voice shaking.

"Nope, we don't like it," agreed Tommy.

Rachel smiled and her heart swelled with happiness. She gazed at Jeffrey. "You called me Mama. That's the first time."

Tommy took a bite of pancake. "You our mama now." Not a question in his voice just a statement.

She smiled at her sons. "That's right, and you are my children. You and Jeffrey are my sons, and Maggie and Gertie are my daughters." Rachel turned her gaze toward Maggie.

The girl grinned and nodded. "Can we call you Mama, now?"

Rachel's eyes filled with tears. She'd waited so long for this to happen. "Yes, yes, of course. Nothing in this world would make me happier."

Maggie frowned. "Mama, don't cry." She went over to Rachel.

She had regained her chair at the table.

Her daughter put her arms around her shoulders and hugged her. "We're awfully glad you came."

"So am I." She looked toward Joshua and held out a hand.

He walked to her and brought it to his lips where he kissed the top. "Maggie couldn't have said it better. We, all of us, are very glad you decided to marry me."

"I can't imagine any life where I'm not here. I love you." She hugged Maggie tighter. "All of you."

Joshua kissed her.

She didn't wish for anything else. All of her dreams came true when she became the Carson City marshal's bride.

EPILOGUE

June 6, 1862

Rachel lit a lamp and then, holding the small of her back, she walked and walked around the kitchen. She tried to be quiet, but sometimes a moan escaped.

Joshua came in, his hair sticking out all over. "How long have you been up? Now is when you usually come to bed. You need to see Doc about this lack of sleep you're experiencing."

She leaned into his chest.

He put his arms around her shoulders.

She stayed in his arms, soaking up his strength, for as long as she could. Then she had to pull away.

"At least, when the baby comes, which hopefully will be soon, I'll already be used to not sleeping."

He chuckled. "I guess that's one way of looking at it."

"I think it's time to send Maggie for the doctor."

Joshua eased her out of his arms and looked at her, eyes wide. "Now? Are you sure?"

Rachel smiled. "I'm pretty sure. My water broke about three hours ago, and I just feel like it's time. My labor pains are coming closer and closer together."

"Okay. I'll wake her. She was almost too excited to sleep. She'll probably jump out of bed and run to the doctor's in her nightgown."

"At this point, I'd run to the doctor in my nightgown…if I could run. Is the bed ready…the oilcloth under the sheet?"

"Yes, we did that last night, remember?"

"Of course." She sighed. "I can't think of anything but the pain. It's strange. It's only in my back. I expected it to be in my stomach."

"Why don't you lie down for a while?"

"That position hurts my back too much. I will when the doctor gets here."

"Which won't happen if I don't get Maggie. I'll be right back."

Joshua left the kitchen.

Rachel paced again…'round and 'round the room…anything that would ease the pain. She heard the front door slam and knew Maggie was on her way.

Joshua returned to the kitchen. "Shall I walk with you? We can walk around the outside of the house, if you want."

"No, I don't think so. I feel like I'm too close."

After she'd paced for another ten or fifteen minutes, Joshua by her side, the front door slammed again.

"Doc's here," yelled Maggie.

Rachel and Joshua headed for the living room.

"Hi, Doc," said Joshua.

"Hi, Doc. Are you ready to deliver my baby? Because I don't think it will be long now."

"Hi, to both of you. Rachel, you need to lie down so I can take a look and see how far along you are."

"Okay." She waddled back to the bedroom and lay on Joshua's side of the bed. She raised her knees and opened them wide.

"Joshua, open the curtains please, and hold the lamp down here for me. I need plenty of light."

Once her husband completed those tasks, Doc began the exam.

"Well, what have we here? Your little one is definitely ready to be born. I'm glad you didn't go outside to walk. Your baby is crowning, and now you'll help him by pushing. Ready?"

"Yes. That's all I want to do, anyway."

"I'm ready to catch your infant, so now is the time. Push, Rachel. Push now."

She pushed and pushed then rested. She pushed again and again until she felt the head slide out. The intense need to push subsided and she caught her breath.

"Very good," said Doc. "Just a little more. We have to get the rest of him out now. Push again."

Again she strained to get her baby the rest of the way. Finally, she felt the infant slide from her body.

Though she was breathing heavily, Rachel tried to sit up but was too tired to manage it. "Well, Doc, what do we have?"

Doc smiled over the towel-wrapped bundle in his arms. "You have a beautiful baby girl, with hair as red as her mama's."

Joshua kissed her forehead. "You did great, although, next time I'll send for Ruth to assist."

Doc took the baby to the bureau and cleaned her up, then he swaddled her in the little blanket Rachel had placed there. He carried the infant to the bed and laid her in Rachel's waiting arms.

She immediately opened the blanket so she and Joshua could see the baby. Rachel waited so long to have a baby of her own. She touched her little fingernails, ran her finger around the delicate shell of her ear, and touched her button nose.

Joshua counted fingers and toes. He placed his finger in one of her hands, and she clasped onto it. He turned to Rachel and smiled. "They always do that, and every time I fall more in love with my baby. I know it's just a reflex, but I love it, anyway."

"You should get the children so they can meet their sister. Well, after we decide her name."

Joshua kept his gaze on the baby. "I thought we were calling her Jennifer?"

"I was thinking we might call her Cassandra, Cassie for short. Cassie Egan. What do you think?"

"I like it. Looks like Cassie it is."

"Good. Now you can get the children."

Doc finished packing his bag. "I'll send them in on my way out."

Joshua finally looked up. "Thanks, Doc. What do I owe you?"

"Attending the birth is included in the payments you've made for the office calls."

Joshua reached out his hand. "Thanks, Doc."

Doc picked up his bag and then shook Joshua's hand. "You all enjoy your little one."

She nodded. "We will, Doc."

He left and for a moment she and Joshua were alone with Cassie. Rachel looked up at Joshua and saw a look on his face which was absolute adoration. It was the same look she probably wore.

A short while later she heard the kids running down the hall.

Maggie, carrying Gertie, was the first in the room. "What do I have, a baby brother or sister?"

"A sister." Joshua smiled. "And slow down. No need to run, she's not going anywhere."

The boys ran, not heeding their father.

"Baby. We want to see the baby," shouted Jeffrey.

Joshua put his finger over his lips. "Keep your voice down."

Jeffrey hung his head. "Sorry."

Rachel smiled. "That's okay, sweetie. Joshua, take her so all the kids can see her."

Gertie pointed at Cassie. "Baba."

Her mother grinned. "That's right, Gertie. Baby. Her name is Cassandra, but we are calling her Cassie."

"Sassie," said Gertie.

"No, honey. Cassie. Say Cassie." Maggie turned Gertie's face toward her. "Say Cassie."

Gertie pointed at the baby. "Sassie."

Maggie sighed. "We'll work on it. Cassie has red hair. I bet it'll be as pretty as yours, Mama."

Rachel's heart swelled and even after six months she still got a thrill each time one of her children called her Mama. It took so long for them to use the name, but the time was worth the result.

She looked up at Joshua.

He smiled. "Happy?"

She ran a finger gently over her daughter's cheek. "I guess you could say that. Ecstatic is more like it. I never dreamed I could be this happy." Rachel looked up into the chocolate brown eyes of her husband. "I love you, Joshua. Thank you for giving me my dreams, my children and you."

"I love you, forever."

Rachel reached out and clasped his hand, then brought her palm flush with his. "Forever and a day."

ABOUT THE AUTHOR

Cynthia Woolf is an award-winning and best-selling author of fifty-five historical western romance novels and six sci-fi romance novels, which she calls westerns in space. Along with these books she has also published five boxed sets of her books. The Tame Series, Destiny in Deadwood, The Marshals Mail Order Brides, Centauri Series and Swords and Blasters.

Cynthia loves writing and reading romance. Her first western romance Tame A Wild Heart was inspired by the story her mother told her of meeting Cynthia's father on a ranch in Creede, Colorado. Although Tame A Wild Heart takes place in Creede that is the only similarity between the stories. Her father was a cowboy, not a bounty hunter, and her mother was a nursemaid (called a nanny now), not the owner of the ranch.

Cynthia credits her wonderfully supportive husband Jim and her great critique partners for saving her sanity and allowing her to explore her creativity.

STAY CONNECTED!

Newsletter

Sign up for my newsletter and get a free book.

Follow Cynthia

https://www.facebook.com/cindy.woolf.5

https://twitter.com/CynthiaWoolf

http://cynthiawoolf.com

ALSO BY CYNTHIA WOOLF

Heart Wish series

Heart of Stone

Heart of Shadow

Heart of Silver

Bachelors and Babies

Carter

Cupids & Cowboys

Lanie

The Marshal's Mail Order Brides

The Carson City Bride

The Virginia City Bride

The Silver City Bride

The Eureka City Bride

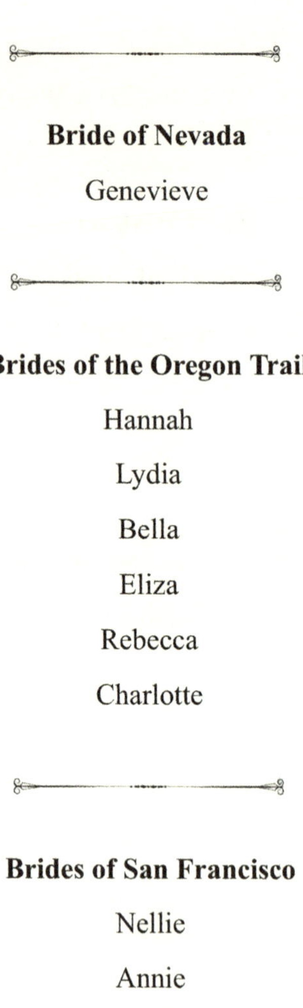

Bride of Nevada

Genevieve

Brides of the Oregon Trail

Hannah

Lydia

Bella

Eliza

Rebecca

Charlotte

Brides of San Francisco

Nellie

Annie

Cora

Sophia

Amelia

Brides of Seattle

Mail Order Mystery

Mail Order Mayhem

Mail Order Mix-Up

Mail Order Moonlight

Mail Order Melody

Brides of Tombstone

Mail Order Outlaw

Mail Order Doctor

Mail Order Baron

Central City Brides

The Dancing Bride

The Sapphire Bride

The Irish Bride

The Pretender Bride

Destiny in Deadwood

Jake

Liam

Zach

Hope's Crossing

The Stolen Bride

The Hunter Bride

The Replacement Bride

The Unexpected Bride

Matchmaker & Co Series

Capital Bride

Heiress Bride

Fiery Bride

Colorado Bride

Troubled Bride

The Surprise Brides

Gideon

Tame

Tame a Wild Heart

Tame a Wild Wind

Tame a Wild Bride

Tame A Honeymoon Heart

Tame Boxset

Centauri Series (SciFi Romance)

Centauri Dawn

Centauri Twilight

Centauri Midnight

Singles

Sweetwater Springs Christmas

Made in the USA
Monee, IL
19 October 2021

80339674R00114